HE HAD ME SECURELY
HIM.

There was no give to his body. His left arm, like a strong metal vise, was slung around in front of me; it and its accompanying hand pinioned my arms against my sides. His belly ground my butt. His chin wedged over my left shoulder, against my neck; his whisker-stubbled right cheek exerted pressure that kept my head from shaking off his other slab-like hand that anchored over my face.

"Don't fight me, damn it!" A whispered command against my left ear.

I had no choice but to struggle. My brain, deprived of oxygen, sent instructions for survival that didn't include passive resistance. I was suffocating in the airless vacuum between his hand and my face.

"I really, really, really liked this one!"
— Joey, DIARY OF A HUSTLER

"A genuinely great read!"
— Alex Von Mann, SLAVES

Other books by WILLIAM MALTESE

CALIFORNIA CREAMIN'
an anthology
ISBN 1902644042

SUMMER SWEAT
an anthology
ISBN 1902644107

A SLIP TO DIE FOR

A STUD DRAQUAL MYSTERY
WILLIAM MALTESE

LAMBERT III LIBRARY
for
PROWLER BOOKS

A Slip to Die For (a Stud Draqual mystery) by William Maltese

ISBN 0-9672420-0-2

First printing September 1999
Cover photography © 1999 William J. Lambert III

Lambert III Library book published by
LAMBERT III LAAGER USA for
PROWLER BOOKS
3 Broadbent Close London N6 5GG

Web-site: prowler.co.uk

Printed in Finland by Werner Soderstrom Oy.

Prologue

The bullet-punched black silk slip was a sensuous lake beached across the shore of the corpse's muscled thighs; the exposed length of flaccid penis placid and calm on its raft of coarse dark hair.

The silk was Draqualian, the end product of a sophisticated and very exclusive manufacturing operation in upstate New York where ravenous silkworms gobble mulberry leaves treated with a secret formula and then excrete gossamer strands of protein in every color of the rainbow.

Draqualian silk is exorbitantly expensive, but Don deZinn could afford the exorbitantly expensive. As that cross-dresser, model, underground movie star, and high-class call-boy confessed to me on more than one occasion: "Stud, I've come a long way since I walked the streets and peddled my cock and ass to the highest bidder."

There was one other interesting thing about that silk slip. It was one of mine.

Chapter One

The death of Gerald Kaney, his corpse decked out in bullet-riddled slip of red Draqualian, was what in the final shakeout actually put my name and product before the public and inspired the million-dollar slogan, Lingerie to Die For! Not that I hadn't gotten my fair share of publicity when Don deZinn ended his much-publicized life in a black Stud Draqual creation which had been pre-sold to him prior to its appearance in my Summer-Fall catalog.

What was even more attention-getting about Gerald – as if the very thought of Gerald Kaney dressed in a women's red slip hadn't been enough – was that few people, myself among them, would have expected him to be found dead, quite literally, wearing Catalog Item #X1456 since it, too, had been pre-sold to Don deZinn. It was the "Women's Wear Daily" star reporter, Henry

Kleff, who connected the red to the black; and it didn't take long after that until Inspector John O'Reilly, New York Police Department, Detective Branch, came knocking on my office door.

"Mr. Stud..." He paused as if in stunned incredulity. "Draqual, is it?" He was in his early 40's, not particularly well-dressed, but no slouch either. Slightly ravaged. Handsome in his way: square jaw, cleft chin, vertically carved left cheek. Sometime in the past he'd had that dreaded one drink too many, and the effects since then had been cumulative.

He flashed the photographs of Gerald's cold, very dead, very red-silk clad body, and wanted to know if Mr. Kaney had been gay.

People often make the false assumption – and O'Reilly was apparently no exception – that any man, like I, in the lingerie business simply had to have wide knowledge of all the sexual perversities of which human beings are capable and particularly those of the most aberrant and kinkiest sort. They would never believe I had come into the business screaming and kicking in protest. I'd scarred my slender body and fragile mind for years proving my manhood and trying to live down my father's success as the most innovative producer and purveyor of female underwear in the business. It was polo, that princely but rugged sport, that turned out to be the final outlandish macho endeavor which put me in the hospital, and as the crooners would have it, "done me in".

"Wouldn't you be surer of a correct answer to that question from Gerald's ex?" That's how I saw it.

"I'll talk to her, rest assured. In the meantime..."

I cut him off by launching into a lengthy and graphically detailed dissertation on the differences and similarities among gay, homosexual, queer, fag, transsexual, nancy, transvestite, drag, and cross-dresser. But this cop had been around the block too many times and had seen more than enough of his share of the bent and crooked to be shaken by anything I might say to embarrass him. He simply and quite literally ignored me.

Meeker and more humbled than I would care to admit, I summed up my little lecture by finally telling him that, as far as I knew, Gerald's sex life was no kinkier – and probably less so – than some of the stuff he, O'Reilly, had no doubt bumped up against in his long and illustrious career with the N.Y.P.D.

Not that I was privy to Gerald's bedroom secrets. All I had to go on was the talk. There was always plenty of that!, and, yes, the few times when we had found ourselves in the same grunting and groaning dog pile which, if the various components had been sifted and labeled according to sex, wouldn't necessarily have turned up being of the correct male-to-female ratio every time. That had been during the eighties, when even the most macho heterosexual cocksman couldn't always tell, via the Braille method, what was what and who was whom among all those bodies slipping and sliding on Crisco-ed rubber sheets in some dark room.

O'Reilly then wanted to know if Mr. deZinn had ever been interested (I found his euphemism a bit quaint), in Gerald Kaney.

The only thing I was sure of was that Don had experienced more than his share of brotherly love. He'd been a hustler, after all, and had never made any bones about it. And the gay scene had been very much a part of his business, even after he had moved on to bigger and better things. "It would have to be a pretty damn big dick," Don had told me, once, "to top some I've seen in my time."

"Or didn't he consider Mr. Kaney, uh, shall we say, sufficiently endowed?" Obviously O'Reilly was aware of the gossip around town that Don had been a size-queen.

"Is there anyone between Earth and Betelgeuse who didn't consider Gerald well-hung?" I'd played squash with Gerald more than once and had seen him in the showers enough times to know what I knew. For someone like myself who believed himself to have been definitely short-changed in the cock department, Gerald had been the brunt of a helluva lot of size-envy. Not that I told O'Reilly any of this.

"I mean..." O'Reilly didn't bother to finish. He tapped one of the photos. The picture was proof enough that Gerald had not only been hung like a horse, but had also chosen a Draqualian slip far too short to conceal his giant-size manhood. Don's crotch, as well as Gerald's, had been airbrushed from sight in all the subsequent supermarket checkout-counter tabloids.

"As far as I know, the relationship between Gerald and Don was strictly business."

O'Reilly wasn't about to let that slide. "As far as you know?"

"Yes."

"But a sexual thing was possible?"

The cop was making me defensive and uneasy. My supercilious grin was aimed deliberately at giving him the impression that I knew there are some pretty strange people out there, among whom he could consider himself, who are more turned on by hearing about it than doing it.

"Well?"

"Anything's possible," I said. Too bad Don wasn't alive to give O'Reilly the nitty-gritty. Don had not only been a walking encyclopedia of clinical body functions, but could – and would, too, when of a mind – expound upon them at length and with great expertise.

"O.K. then, what about their business relationship?"

"Don thought it was time to let the eagerly-awaiting world know what kind of life he'd led," I replied, "and a couple of big-name publishers were interested. Trouble was, he couldn't write for shit. But his life story was juicy enough to have pushed to the top of any best-seller list and stayed there." Maybe O'Reilly figured it was one or more of those juicy bits that had gotten Don killed – maybe even had gotten Gerald killed. "Telaman Press won the bidding war."

"Gerald was Don's ghostwriter?" There was no need to ask me. O'Reilly knew better, but I played along with his little game of double- checking, triple-checking, quadruple-checking, however-many checking each and every little piece of information which had been fed him during the course of the investigation. I was smart enough to know that something might eventually click and hand the police the one clue necessary to solve two murders. And I noted O'Reilly's switch to first names, too, and wondered why he was beginning to feel cozy.

"Gerald wasn't a writer, either. His forte was looking great in front of a TV camera."

I had always figured the brass had done itself a very bad turn when they kicked Gerald's ass upstairs to Vice President of Production; so had a lot of the all-important Nielsen-rating families who abandoned the network like rats off a sinking ship. There had been talk that Gerald was going back on the air; however, instead of taking what would have been a serious gamble, the network recruited handsome Mr. Phil Metcalf from an L.A. affiliate to fill Gerald's spot and to lure back the fickle, broken-hearted viewers.

"Stan Greenlyne was ghosting," I continued in answer to O'Reilly's question.

Stan Greenlyne had started his literary career by writing dirty books – one, sometimes two, a month – for a soft-porn publisher out of San Diego. From there, he'd graduated to romances, writing under the pseudonym Pamela Dreen. He'd then formed his own publishing house, Telaman Press, and under the aegis of his own imprint had ghostwritten Telaman's first best-seller, CONFESSIONS OF A RED DESOTA. This was the autobiography of an Indian kid who had slept his way off the reservation and into some of the biggest and most important beds in Hollywood. The Telaman Press publication of CONFESSIONS... had coincided with the four-hundred-ninety-something anniversary of

Columbus' discovery of the New World, or – as the United Federation of American Indigenous Peoples put it – "the anniversary of the exploitation and annihilation of the red man by the white". Not as knock-them-dead publicity as Lingerie to Die For!, but pretty damned good, nonetheless. With its growing backlist of mega-sellers, Telaman Press was now a money-making machine of tremendous power. It had become somewhat of a phenomenon in the business and was looked upon as a cash cow by more than one of the older, more prestigious, more established, less lucrative houses.

Don deZinn's life story was to have been Telaman Press' next and biggest blockbuster.

"So, what's the connection between Gerald and Don?" asked O'Reilly.

"Aside from their mutual good taste in lingerie?" I quipped.

O'Reilly, probably like Queen Victoria, did not find this amusing. "Aside from their possible connection in the bedroom."

He waited patiently to hear what he and I both knew he already knew.

"Don had met Gerald on a TV talk show," I replied. "He liked him. Sexually? Maybe, but not necessarily. Don didn't bed everyone he liked." I was a prime example, but that was none of O'Reilly's business. "All Don knew about Stan Greenlyne in the beginning was that Stan had won the high-stakes bidding war to ghostwrite and publish his life story. As it turned out, when he had gotten to know Stan a little better, he didn't like him. 'A gross bully!' he said. Eventually, Don talked Gerald into acting as sounding board and liaison. The arrangement was that Don would tell his story to Gerald, via tape recorder, and then Gerald would hand over the notes and tapes to Stan. Stan would relay to Gerald what holes needed filling."

O'Reilly actually smiled. A dirty old man after all, despite his squeaky-clean image.

"Gerald the middleman." Succinct and right on the button. No dullard, this cop. "And Gerald's alcohol problem?"

"What about it?" I asked.

"He did have one, didn't he?" O'Reilly was pushing me, and he knew it.

"Did he?" I'd been with my shrink long enough to know about avoiding a question by asking one.

"You tell me."

"Would you define alcohol problem?" I was feeling obstinate, but O'Reilly didn't give even the vaguest hint that I might be getting to him.

"Would you say he drank more than normal? More than you, for example." O.K.! So, O'Reilly had already heard of each and every one of my fall-down drunks.

"I have a low liquor threshold," I said.

"Did Gerald? Or do you think the stories about his being kicked upstairs at the network because of his drinking are exaggerated?" And crafty, too, nailing me with a sudden veer to the present tense like that.

I finessed the question: "I did hear rumors to that effect."

"How about Gerald and Kenneth Salmoth... the talk?"

Ken Salmoth had been a well-fed, well-heeled stockbroker who took a very high-profile dive off a very well-known New York City landmark and didn't survive to tell the tale. Suspicions of embezzlement had circulated around town, but they had all been proven unwarranted in the end. No one seemed to know just why Ken had chucked in the good life.

"What talk?"

"That Kenneth Salmoth and Gerald were both one of the boys."

"This cop's persistence with cute euphemisms was getting to me, and I'd had just about enough. "Ken Salmoth never told me Gerald fucked him, or vice-versa, if that's what you mean. Is this going to take much longer? I have work to do."

O'Reilly surprised me. He stood. "There are probably more questions I'll have for you later on. But for now I want to thank you for your cooperation. See you around, Mr. Draqual."

After he had closed the door behind him, I crossed my office to the wet bar and poured a large scotch, took a hefty swallow, and didn't stop shuddering until the taste had burned its way down. I hated the stuff, but God knows I'd drunk enough of the very, very best in thousands of unsuccessful attempts to acquire a taste. It never happened.

I dumped what was left down the sink and poured myself a small pony of creme de cacao. I like creme de cacao. I like creme de menthe. I like Grand Marnier. When given a choice, and feeling confident enough of my manhood, I opt for the tutti-frutti, umbrella-laden concoctions every time.

I glanced at my reflection in the mirror behind the bottles, decanters, and Baccarat crystal. My facial features were too finely chiseled; eyelashes too thick, too dark, and too long; eyes too purple; lips too bee-stung. My physique beneath the form-fitting Brioni suit wasn't bulky enough to warrant the moniker my well-intentioned father had saddled me with – Stud, for Christ's sake!

Long hours of weight training had never made a hill-of-beans difference; and on rare occasions, I had contemplated steroids and still did.

Also beneath my suit, my too-small dick.

I rationalized: If, in addition to having feminine good looks and a father who looked like a linebacker but had made his name in women's lingerie, I had been possessed of a killer-sized whang, God only knows how much more fucked up I might have been.

Chapter Two

Dr. Melissa DoLittle had come highly recommended, and I'd liked the name Melissa. I knew the stories about shrinks who take advantage of their clients' vulnerability to trick them into hot sex, and I'd wanted to avoid any Dr. Butch Getum or Dr. Hunk Craven. As it turned out, Dr. Melissa was in her sixties and, except for hanging on to the few patients she couldn't dump, or they'd likely blow their brains out, had been trying to fade into retirement for years. I'd squeezed in through the door only because my father – this was before he died – was King of Silk Nighties, and Dr. Melissa hadn't been able to pass up the opportunity for a Draqualian silk teddy at cost. Or so she had confessed during one of our later sessions wherein she shared one secret with me for every one I shared with her.

Dr. Melissa was convinced, as she still is, that when the murders of Don deZinn and Gerald Kaney exploded on my world, I suddenly began to see myself metamorphosed into an amalgam of every real and fictionalized detective. I'd been forced to give up polo and mountain climbing and shooting the rapids when, as I was about to make a game-winning goal, my pony stumbled and dumped me beneath the clattering hooves of three horses; hence, my ensuing in-depth involvement in the investigation of the murders was, according to Dr. Melissa, yet only another male-oriented hobby which would prove once and for all, and to whomever still wondered about my sexuality (There were more than a few!) that Stud Draqual only pulled down his pants for the ladies.

I tried to explain to Dr. Melissa that the investigation business was too rife with the likes of Miss Marples and Jessica Fletchers to be a legitimate vehicle for proving my manhood. Circumstances, cruel fate, happenstance, and plain bad luck were what had sucked me in, pure and simple.

The first bit of bad luck was when Kyle Kaiser didn't show up for work. This didn't mean all that much at the time. Kyle was a fitter. I knew who he was and that he was good at his job, but that was about it. The lingerie business, like any other, has its attention-getters, but Kyle wasn't one of them.

Not that fitters were/are unimportant. As easy as it is for people to think it's no big deal for a woman to slip into a simple bit of silk and strut some runway, it takes a lot of pinning and tucking to make an original Stud Draqual teddy or chemise look form-fitting on models who come in all shapes and sizes. And nobody's going to land that final four-digit sale if a Stud Draqual is pockmarked with needle holes. Kyle Kaiser was very good at keeping it neat and clean.

So although Kyle was a member of my little Draqualian family, I didn't know he had ever been involved with Don deZinn, except for the one or two times he had fit Don's heavily defined masculine angles into a clinging piece of Draqualian underwear. As I was to discover much later, the only person at Draqual Fashions, except Kyle himself, of course, who knew differently, was Betty Meiken, my assistant. She'd seen Kyle and Don kissing in Fitting Cubicle J; but as she herself hadn't been noticed, and was liberal enough to remember with genuine fondness her own first passionate kiss from a female roommate during her student days at UCLA, she'd kept their little secret to herself.

After Don's murder and Kyle's no-show, and if possibly she'd had the time, Betty might have thought about the connection between the two events. As it was, she'd been busy lining up a replacement for Kyle and anxiously keeping everything coordinated for an invitation-only fashion show.

The show wasn't one of our big spring or fall extravaganzas but a small private affair for twelve very special customers. Lady Helen Thomas had flown in from London for the occasion. That Greta Kaney would make the numbered guest list an unlucky thirteen was something I didn't know until it was too late.

I'd met Greta Kaney socially once or twice but had run into her only occasionally since then. That I'd seen Gerald around town more often without his wife in tow probably said a lot about their marriage.

Gerald was seldom alone. There was always someone hovering and, if not with him officially, playing female moth to his male flame. If O'Reilly was right about Gerald's hanky-panky with the "boys", as he called them, that was something Gerald had never flaunted in front of me or anyone else that I knew of. He couldn't afford to. His adoring viewers would have paled at the notion of their favorite TV newsman doing dirties in his or in any other handsome man's bedroom. Gerald loved his job and wanted to keep it.

"Mrs. Kaney on line one, Mr. Draqual," was how Betty announced Greta's call. (Not even Betty called me by my first name, at least not to my face and certainly not in the hearing of potential buyers of a Draqual original. Betty had class, and Stud just would not do). I picked up the phone.

"Harriet?!" It was my mistake, not Betty's.

Harriet Haney, wife of Dallas banker Darrel Haney, called at least once a year, just before her husband's birthday, when she wanted another little something to rev Darrel's ancient and recalcitrant engine.

"I understand you're having a show this afternoon," sounding strangely unlike the old Harriet Haney I knew quite well and liked intensely. Harriet is in her early seventies and sounds like a gin-soaked, smoke-befogged meat grinder. I'd once remarked that God must have been having a bad day when he assigned us our respective voice boxes. If I didn't concentrate on a decidedly deep-throated "Hello!" when I answered the phone, strangers often mistook me for a miss, a Ms., or, more likely, a Mrs. Where Harriet is usually mistaken for a Mr. Early in our acquaintance she'd told me she thought my voice "very sexy, Stud!" But even I, out to prove something in those days by screwing anything with two legs and tits, who had a pulse and breathed, was astute enough to realize this was no sexual come-on. Harriet was just... well, Harriet.

Some quick mental arithmetic told me that Darrel

Haney's birthday was still a long way off.

"Just a few friends in for a little look-see and some bubbly," I told the caller. I'd long since learned how to deal with the weird types – men, women, and in-betweens – who crash fashion shows and thrill and tickle themselves by ogling half-naked women parading a runway.

"I'd like very much to stop by." Definitely not Harriet. Definitely not a rusty meat grinder clunking away, but a clear, concise, New England finishing school purr. "Would that be possible?"

I played it cool and capitalized on my mistake. "I would have had an invitation to you in a minute had I known you were in the City."

"I am sorry this is so last-minute."

"But then you're an old customer, Harriet, and you know I can squeeze you in anytime." I charged ahead. "By the way, how did your husband like that cream-colored, lace-trimmed number?"

Brief silence, and then...

"I'm afraid you must have me confused with someone else, Mr. Draqual." I'd expected her to continue her bluff and was surprised by her candor.

"I'm dreadfully sorry," I said. "I could have sworn my assistant said Harriet Haney."

"Actually, Mr. Draqual, it's Kaney. Greta Kaney. We've met a couple of times, but perhaps this is too much of an imposition. I'm looking for something to give me a mental lift, you know? Silvia Karkman said one of your originals does it for her every time."

"I remember you very well, Mrs. Kaney, and apologize again for not recognizing your voice. I'll see that your name is on the list. If you can arrange to be here about two." No way was I going to pass up a chance to find out how Greta Kaney was weathering her ex-husband's murder. Dr. Melissa would have said I was playing detective again.

"Yes. Thank-you. I do appreciate it."

I'd no sooner hung up and was mulling over whether Greta Kaney's self-invitation might, indeed, go beyond her need for a simple pick-me-up when Stan Greenlyne called.

No mistaking the voice this time, or Stan's sense of the macabre.

"Since Draqualian silk slips seem to be in, these days, I was wondering what you could do for me in something wondrously canary?"

He seemed inordinately cheerful for someone whose Telaman Press had just lost out on a potential best-seller. Then again, maybe Gerald and Don had managed to provide Telaman Press with enough material to complete the book. Maybe Stan had killed them both so he wouldn't have to share the profits, profits that would be far greater than expected in the wake of all the hype about the murders. Except Gerald, mere sounding board and liaison would have gotten only a flat fee, and that certainly was not motive enough for murder. Or, was it? Stud, boy detective, hard at work, I mentally slapped my own face to bring me back to reality.

"For a good fit, we might have to add several side panels," I replied. Stan was hefty-size. "It'll quadruple the cost of the piece, but a Draqualian silk slip is worth it."

He laughed. To my ear, a rather pleasant laugh, but Don always said it sounded like a "bad case of gas coming out the wrong blow-hole." Don hadn't liked the idea that a man who once wrote dirty books for the porno trade had won the bidding war to co-author and publish his autobiography. In my experience people from the bottom only rarely appreciate others who have clawed their way to the top as well. Somehow the accomplishment is diluted by every new arrival.

"I was hoping we could have lunch," Stan said. I was going to say something about last-minute, but he beat me to it. "I know this is short notice, but it's important – for me. About this mess with Don deZinn and Gerald Kaney, don't you know?"

I should have backed off right then and there, but maybe Dr. Melissa was right after all. Maybe I really was out to crack the case. I'd known Don, and I'd known Gerald. Maybe I actually knew the murderer, and Stan could offer a few helpful hints.

"Sorry, Stan, but I've an important group of clients coming in at two." Should I name-drop Greta Kaney?

"I'm in my car, only a couple of blocks away."

I vacillated. "O.K., then, but it will have to be some place close-by."

"Rodney's?"

It was close. It was new. It was expensive. Getting reservations was a bear. The food was superb. I was hooked.

"I can manage only an hour, tops," I replied.

"I'll be out front in five minutes."

When I stepped out of my building, I found Stan already on the sidewalk and ready to greet me.

"Nice of you to make time," he said.

His handshake was the bear-grip I remembered. Still squeezing, he put his free arm around my back and expertly steered me to his waiting limo as easily as if we were on a dance floor.

The liveried chauffeur was there to open the door.

The bullet was faster than we were. It dimpled the shiny black leather upholstery with a hollow-sound thud.

Chapter Three

As an active and enthusiastic participant in the most strenuous and he-man of sports and adventures, before being permanently knocked out of commission on the polo field, no one had ever exactly called me a klutz, at least not within hearing; and I'd come through it all without too many visual scars. Admittedly, there were just enough telltale cicatrices, to be found on my left eyebrow, right forearm, and left knee, to make bed-talk interesting; but there were not enough of them to indicate that I'd ever been overly clumsy. Because of some quick defensive maneuvers I'd somehow managed to bring off once I hit the turf, even the wounds inflicted by the polo accident had healed to cosmetic perfection. But all of my famed agility came to naught when it was, this time, quite literally, a case of my possible death by gunfire.

I'd been shot at – or at least thought I had – and was not what anyone would call particularly swift. I did not pull myself, Stan, his chauffeur, or any and all innocent bystanders out of any possible follow-up line of fire. I did not turn toward the gunman and charge him with the kind of incorporated evasive tactics which would have made Joe Football proud of me, an elusive moving target. I did not put the full force of my muscled poundage mid-center to the culprit's breadbasket, thereby deflating his gut and his ability to continue blasting away. I did not keep the bastard pinned securely to the ground while someone less heroic than I dialed 911. What I did do was freeze as solid as a Mafia rat fink fast-hardened in cement. What's more, I stayed there, even as my brain kept flashing its urgent warning: "You've been shot at, and it would be far better if you hauled ass!"

It was Stan and his chauffeur who quickly and expertly extracted us from this insane street-corner dilemma. As I found later, their coordinated effort had been born of experience. Apparently, this was not the first time someone had taken a potshot at Stan and missed. Publishing was doubtlessly a dangerous business for a man who had made his fame and fortune by sullying people's reputations and airing dirty laundry which many felt better left buried in fetid hampers.

I'd seen well-muscled quarterbacks slower on their feet than this very fat man who propelled himself, ahead of me, into the car, grabbed me by the lapels, jerked me unceremoniously into the backseat after him, and buried my face in the protective cushioning of his extremely wide and comforting belly.

"Sorry about that," he apologized.

The chauffeur – I don't know even yet how he managed it – hopped in behind the wheel, and the car shot forward with a momentum that slammed the open backdoor shut with a deep heavy bang.

"I was afraid something like this might happen," Stan said as the car picked up speed and relocated itself amidst traffic which had been scattered by the gunfire. I lifted my flushed face a few inches to free myself from Stan's smothering crotch.

"Funny, but I was taken completely by surprise," I replied with as much forced sarcasm as I could manage.

Stan didn't seem to notice. His mind was on other things. "Mildred would be more than a little unhappy if Clem had accidentally left her favorite lingerie-maker dead on some doorstep," he said.

"Mildred who? Clem?" Somewhere in my subconscious, a couple of little bells tinkled away; but at the moment, I was more interested in catching my breath, and basking in relief that I had come out of all this in one piece, than in sorting out two names from among the thousands stored in my mental Rolodex. Stan didn't elaborate.

"You look none the worse for wear," he finally said. His massive hands once again took me by the lapels and, this time, gently pulled me to a more fully upright position. "How did that adrenaline rush compare to that of, say, mountain climbing?" Polite conversation at a time like this? I wasn't interested.

"Who was that...?" I was going to say "masked man", but the features of the man who had fired at us were still muted behind a kaleidoscopic blur; and he hadn't been wearing a mask at all (better to meld into the foot traffic?). Disorientation obviously still had me in its clutches, and my heart was continuing to pound away considerably faster than its normal rate.

"I thought I'd said who it was." Stan sounded as if my denseness was purposely on the other side of lead. "One of Clem Rollins' hoods."

"Clem Rollins? Mildred Rollins?" My cranial cavity erupted with the tintinnabulation of the finale of the "1812 Overture".

"Jesus, Stan! Surely not because of some book you're about to publish." I could see copies of UNDERWORLD EXPOSED pyramided in a bookstore display window shattered by Clem Rollins' hired-and-paid-for machine-gun fire.

"Give me some credit, Stud," Stan said. "I have enough trouble steering clear of rank amateurs without inviting the pros to the party."

Which didn't explain Clem Rollins' responsibility for the little to-do in front of my building.

"I seem to be missing something," I said.

"It'll become clearer over lunch."

"Lunch?"

"I did invite you to lunch, didn't I? Didn't we agree on Rodney's, because it was close and you had people coming in?" Stan was not a man whose appetite was spoiled by any sudden and miraculous escape from sure and certain death.

The limo pulled up in front of the restaurant, and the doorman opened the door with a "Good to see you again, Mr. Greenlyne." I received a cursory nod and a sterile, unenthusiastic "Mr. Draqual?" The guy was not sure of my name and looked as if he would rather not have ventured a guess. The ceremony was choreographed around dollar signs, of course, and Stan had accumulated several times over more bucks than I'd managed to stash in my admittedly sizable stockpile.

The maitre d' knew me, yes, but that didn't deter him from kissing the ass of the man who would pay the bill and leave the tip. "That private booth you requested, Mr. Greenlyne..."

We were directed through thick curtains which isolated us from the rest of the dining room. Once we were seated, Stan leaned over the table and wafted peppermint-smelling breath in my face. I'd never before thought of him as being overly fastidious about his person.

"Stud, I want you to arrange a meeting between Clem Rollins and me."

I was incredulous and obviously showed it.

"You can do it," Stan insisted. "You're perfect."

"I don't even know Clem Rollins." And I didn't want to know him. He had the reputation of being simultaneously a real charmer and a real snake in a real charmer's basket.

"You won't deny knowing Mildred!"

I hadn't yet settled down from Stan's lead-in. I jumped skittishly when the waiter rapped for our attention before opening the curtains to ask if we were ready to order. Rodney's was well-known for creative cuisine, but I'd stopped being hungry several eons ago when a bullet thudded into the backseat of Stan's limo. I ordered tomato soup, salad, and lime sorbet.

Stan rolled his eyes in resignation, as if to say "O.K.

Don't eat!" His eyes were surprisingly large and unporcine for a man with three chins, their whites unusually clear for someone in the eye-straining book business.

"Leave the menu," Stan instructed the waiter. "I'm sure Mr. Draqual's appetite will catch up with him shortly. In the interim, I'll have..."

I didn't follow the intricacies of Stan's order. The waiter was an expert and needed to make only one small adjustment on his pad when Stan changed his mind about his dessert. "Make that mousse instead of cheesecake, please."

The trough provided for, Stan turned back to me. "Mildred will assure her husband that you can be trusted not to have any clever tricks up your sleeve." Easy for Stan to say.

"If Telaman Press isn't publishing some expose of local crime, why a meeting with Clem Rollins? Why does he have a hired gun out to mow you down?" More importantly, even if I didn't say so: "Why am I dodging bullets which could easily have killed me?"

"The less you know, the better," Stan said, like a prudish papa answering an inquisitive child who'd just asked about sex.

"Wrong!" I said.

No doubt he thought I was being purposely difficult. He sighed like a huge balloon which has suddenly sprung a leak. His whole body jiggled as he settled in for another go at me. His brown eyes rolled upward as if seeking help from whatever deity might reside beyond the stamped-tin ceiling of Rodney's restaurant.

"If I told you," he said as his eyes rolled back downward, one lagging slightly behind, like a recalcitrant tumbler on a Vegas one-armed bandit, "you'd likely find the next bullet coming at you."

"I'd prefer you left me out of this entirely."

His response was delayed by the delivery of the wine. He performed the attending ritual: cork-sniffing and squeezing, wine-fume inhalation, noisy sipping and plentitudinous air-sucking and lip-smacking, ending in an appreciative finale: "Excellent! Excellent!"

"It's to do with the Don deZinn book," Stan confessed once the wine steward had left the table. "Rather with a Don deZinn tape. One I didn't review until after Don's somewhat unfortunate demise."

"End up with enough to salvage the book?" I asked. I admitted to myself there was a mercenary motive behind my question. Few people other than Stan – indeed if anyone else at all – knew how much of the book Don had finished before he was murdered. Enough could mean another Telaman Press best-seller. Which would mean a rise in that company's stock. Which meant that if I could obtain a bit of insider information...!

Stan was noncommittal. "We're still trying to decide."

My look told him that I didn't consider that exactly scratch my back and I'll scratch yours.

"Do you own any Telaman Press stock, Stud? We've done very well for our stockholders, but there are bound to be setbacks in any business."

So much for my enriched stock portfolio. But good deeds for the sake of good deeds are for Boy Scouts earning merit badges, and I'd already lost a few years off my life in the line of fire. I was still ticked that Stan had exposed me to danger without my consent. When subjected to the rigors of polo, mountain climbing, and white-water rafting, I had been so of my own volition and not because someone had dragged me screaming into the melee.

"Do you know how many times Mildred Rollins has suggested I meet her husband?" I asked. "When a brief get-together with him might have been very helpful to Draqual Fashions in clearing up some slight difficulty? And do you know how many times I've side-stepped?" Just because I'd never sat down around the table with

Clem in person didn't mean I was unaware that he probably had his greedy fingers in every rag-business bowl on the Street.

"Which makes you all the more valuable," Stan replied. "Clem knows you've purposely kept clear until now."

Until now? That I didn't like at all.

We were interrupted by a waiter wheeling in six serving trays. My time and patience were both getting pretty short, and I realized I might have to excuse myself before Stan had finished eating. I was wrong. He was not only voracious but fast. He had cut through a duck pate, oysters on the half shell, cream-sauteed mushrooms, three veal cutlets, and a medallion of beef before I had speared my last lettuce leaf.

Stan talked with his mouth full but managed to enunciate perfectly around the grind of his teeth and the pop of his jaw. I perked up considerably when he began to tell me how Don had recorded highly incriminating smut about Clem Rollins which he, Stan, had no intention of ever making public by publishing or otherwise, no sirree! He was only anxious to turn over the tape to Clem – anytime, anywhere. No need for hired hit men, for Christ's sake!

"I wish I'd never heard it," he said. After inhaling the

cheesecake, which he'd decided to order after all, he started on the mousse. "But I did. And immediately forgot it, too. Clem can have the tape. He's welcome to it. I just want him to know of my good intentions. Are you prepared to read in some two-bit newspaper that I got blown away because you, Mr. Stud Draqual of Draqual Fashions, refused to use your acquaintance with Mrs. Rollins to set up a meet? And Stud, you know as well as I do how nosy and resourceful reporters can be. They can find anything!"

I was not as unwilling to mediate with Mildred Rollins as Stan imagined. But it would cost him. "I'll see what I can do," I said.

"Good man! I knew I could count on you; and you can count on me to throw some business your way. I know a lot of rich people."

But would that be enough, though, Stan, old boy? We'd see.

I checked my watch.

"Just ten more minutes while I have my pie," Stan promised. Mousse? Cheesecake? Pie! I would never have believed it if I hadn't seen it with my own eyes. I fiddled with my cutlery while Stan wolfed, but we were finally on our way out of the restaurant in less time than I would have thought possible.

Instinct – and the penchant for self-survival that had failed me when the bullet was flying – did better by me this time. I was immediately suspicious of a man talking to Stan's chauffeur. The chauffeur turned my way as I came out the door, and he nodded at me by way of seeming identification. I took off fast and would still be running if a human tank hadn't stepped from behind a parked truck to assume a legs-wide pose, directly in front of me, each leg bent slightly at its knee, gun in the hand of an extended right arm, left hand gripping right wrist in support, gaping mouth bellowing "Police! Stop right there, or I'll blow you away!"

I'd been offered more than one "blow", in my day, but never one quite so emphatic. And I hadn't even heard his mention of the word "Police!"

Chapter Four

Few things halt a man in his tracks faster than another man with a gun. My brain screamed "Stop!" and my reflexes tried to obey, but there was no way I was going to be able to bring my body to a screeching standstill on the head of a pin.

The man behind the gun stayed anchored to his spot as I lunged those few feet farther toward him. I had no reason to think he wouldn't pull the trigger once I'd become a stationary target. Quite apart from the gun aimed squarely at my gut, his looks didn't make me overly confident that I'd ever walk away from this little bagatelle as a living, breathing human being. He was seedy and rumpled in a suit coat and slacks, shirt open at the collar and roped by a loosely-knotted food-stained knit tie; an eleven-o'clock shadow six hours beyond chic; tired, squinty eyes with heavy mauve-colored bags beneath them.

Would anyone have guessed cop? I didn't. Even after he identified himself in the regulatory way prescribed for all cops when confronted either by enemies or non-enemies in the line of duty, I still had trouble believing him. He looked just too grubby... not that I had any hard-bound idea of how cops were supposed to look. There was no way I could have known his partner and he had been headed in from an all-night, early-morning stakeout when they heard the APB for Stan's limousine over the police channel, spotted the car in front of the restaurant, and moved in for a closer look-see. I was to find out only later that the APB had gone out courtesy of a bystander at the scene of the shooting whose selective memory had subsequently pinpointed the limousine license number as that of the getaway car fleeing the scene of a crime.

I was cooling my heels in the backseat of an unmarked police sedan when O'Reilly yanked open the door and hopped in beside me. Surprise! Surprise!

"Sorry about the rough treatment, Mr. Draqual, but you're a hard man to pin down." He paused, apparently waiting for a response, but I was in no mood to accept apologies or lame attempts at clothes-fitting humor. He sighed. "O.K. Now, let me try to get this straight. Someone tries to gun you down on the sidewalk outside your building. Stan Greenlyne drags you into the safety of his limo. The chauffeur calmly drives you away – to lunch?"

What could I say? It sounded incongruous even to me. "It wasn't all that calmly," I replied.

"Not thinking to use the car phone, or either Greenlyne or your cell phone, to call the police?"

"I wasn't thinking clearly." Obviously! "I'm not shot at every day, you realize. Maybe..." I was going to say "next time" but nixed that as bad luck. No need to tempt demons by summoning them.

O'Reilly was still pushing. "Maybe what?"

"Why don't we see if my lawyer can explain better than I can why an average Joe-Citizen, shot at on a city street, shouldn't be expected to act rationally."

"As you know, Mr. Draqual, this is not an arrest. I just want to straighten out a few little inconsistencies. I hope you don't mind if we continue this conversation in my office at the station. In your business, you must be used to a lot of, uh, beautiful people, shall we say, and there are some photos I'd like you to take a look at."

I shrugged in resignation. What else could I do under the circumstances?

***

My lawyer, Marty Lindquist, was a bit more understanding and tolerant of O'Reilly's line of questioning than I was. Easy for him! Marty was oilily conciliatory. "I think Inspector O'Reilly here will agree," he said, "that the bullet hole in the backseat of Mr. Greenlyne's car makes it quite obvious that either you or Mr. Greenlyne was the intended victim of a shooting."

"I really don't know why we didn't call the police." I suddenly realized that Stan and his chauffeur had been less in possession of their wits than I'd given them credit for.

"It would have been better if you had, but..." Marty shrugged. "I'm sure Mr. O'Reilly will also agree that any competent doctor would confirm that your reaction wasn't in the least extraordinary."

"I've an important showing going on at the office, and I should be there. May I make a call?" My bid for escape.

O'Reilly nodded, shoved his desk phone toward me, and left the room.

After getting Betty on the line, I explained to her where I was and why. She assured me she had everything under control. The gunfire outside the building hadn't been noticed by most of the building's tenants who had realized something was fishy only after police showed up asking questions. Betty hadn't known I was involved in the ruckus, and she was aghast.

"Not to worry, Betty. I'm safe and sound... at least for now." Yeah, safe in O'Reilly's arms, I thought, or at least as safe as one can be coiled in the embrace of a famished boa constrictor.

"Maybe you should think twice from now on before accepting invitations from Stan Greenlyne," was how she put it.

Betty and I went back a long way. She had been assigned to me by my father when my token involvement in the business was sporadic and casual. For years, she roamed the corridors with very little to do officially except baby-sit the errant scion. She'd not wasted her time, however, and, to my later advantage and utter delight, had absorbed just about everything there was to know. By the time I'd finally gotten my ass in high gear, she was invaluable.

"You'll have to make my excuses."

"The ladies will survive," she assured me. "A little notoriety won't hurt business, either." Betty was tough.

"I'm not sure when I'll be able to check back with you. They have mug shots they want me to look at."

I didn't see the point of mug shots, since there was no way I could identify the shooter. Or could I? I hadn't seen him. Or had I? Well, maybe I did see him, but everything had happened too fast, in a blur. I had never been shot at before, and I didn't know who the gunman was. Those two facts kept impressing themselves on my mind. And yet...? Had I recognized the man without realizing it? Had there been something vaguely familiar about him? But where in God's name would I ever have run across him? I didn't mingle with underworld ruffians, and if I paid money into criminal coffers, it was done unknowingly by way of openly-legitimate garbage pick-up fees, truck driver payoffs, and dues to the Blouses, Skirts, and Lingerie Association – all necessary parts of operating a business in the City. To come into closer contact than that with any segment of the gun-toting, ruthless element of the City's organized crime syndicates, one would have had to be involved in a way I wasn't and never had been. If anyone found the gunman's face even vaguely familiar, more than likely it would be Stan. He had been crotch-deep in the porno trade before going legit, and everyone knew who had the final thumbs-up, thumbs-down say-so in that business.

"I'll make excuses and hold the fort," promised Betty. "I do have a Mrs. Greta Kaney without an official invitation."

"God, Betty, I'm sorry. I forgot to alert you. She

called, and I told her to come on in."

"She did rather come across as an elegantly dressed gate-crasher." Betty paused a second. She tended to get a little pedantic when her routine was upset. "Luckily, neither I nor any of the ladies are overly superstitious, but..."

"Superstitious?" I still wasn't up to the fine-tuned mental gymnastics necessary to follow Betty's somewhat baroque reasoning.

Betty took pity on a thought process temporarily gone awry. "She made the thirteenth person at the show. You might think about not tempting fate too often." Betty was always telling me what to think. She was usually right.

Marty signaled to me silently: "Get off the fuckin' phone!"

"Hey, Betty, I've really gotta scoot now. And thanks for your help – as always."

"When O'Reilly gets back, he'll have a few more questions," Marty said after I hung up. "Feel free to answer them unless I step in with an objection. Before he gets here, though, I'm going to ask you something, Stud, and I don't want any bullshit. There isn't anything in all this that you have to hide, is there?"

"Swear to God, Marty!" I waited to be struck by lightning.

He raised a hand to calm me down. "Just a thought! Just a thought! You know that lawyer-client confidentiality applies here?"

"It's like I told you." Well... almost.

O'Reilly rejoined us and started right from the top – again!

"Stan Greenlyne called and asked you for lunch."

"Yes."

"Which he does quite often?"

"Which he does not, and did not, all that often."

So, you had no reason to expect a call from him?"

"No... I mean yes."

"But you immediately accepted his invitation, even though you had an important private showing later this afternoon."

"I knew Don deZinn. I knew Gerald Kaney. Both are dead. Was Stan, the third member of that most illustrious literary triumvirate, soon to be dead as well? He thought I might help."

"How?"

"Clem Rollins' wife is a regular client of mine."

"Clem Rollins?" O'Reilly showed no surprise whatever. I was beginning to admire the bastard.

"Stan thought I could arrange a get-together between Clem and himself." So far, I was running on track.

"Clem Rollins having what to do with any of this?"

"Don deZinn and Clem were once involved."

"Something to do with sex?" unperturbed and very much to the point, even though I'd dropped a heavy clangor right in his lap.

"Involved: exactly how Don put it. He didn't volunteer specifics, and I didn't press him. Put your own spin on it."

"But Stan knows specifics?"

"I think he thinks Clem thinks he knows. Whether or not he knows, you'll have to ask Stan." I hoped I'd come out of that tongue-twister wide-eyed and innocent as a babe.

"Don deZinn relayed the specifics to Stan, via autobiographical tapes and notes, through Gerald Kaney," I continued. "DeZinn and Kaney are now dead. Stan has specifics." A very nice summary, I thought.

"Or Don relayed nothing, but Clem at least assuming he had," I offered an alternative. O'Reilly and I both knew Stan would never own up to possessing an incriminating tape and risking a court order to turn it over to the police. Doing so would not have gone over at all well with Clem Rollins.

"Stan has asked for police protection," O'Reilly informed me.

"Not unreasonable under the circumstances."

"And you?"

"I thought we'd decided the bullet had Stan's name on it."

"Had we?"

"Hadn't we?"

"You knew Don deZinn. You knew Gerald Kaney. Both are dead. You know Stan Greenlyne who's still alive, although through no fault of an incompetent gunman who, if he missed Mr. Greenlyne at such close quarters, couldn't shoot a fish in a barrel."

"Insinuating what?"

O'Reilly shrugged. "I've checked out you and deZinn as being good friends, confidants even. Clem Rollins might think Don told you as much as he told Stan via Gerald Kaney."

I was beginning to feel squeamish.

"You're sure you don't have any specifics?" he pressed.

"My client has already answered that question," Marty interjected.

"I'd like to hear it again."

Marty shrugged consent.

"I have no specifics," I followed through.

A uniformed policeman appeared at the open door and

rapped on the jamb. "Mug shots," he said as he thunked six large binders onto the desk. I waded in.

It's common knowledge that mug shots and driver's license photos are taken by one and the same person. How else to explain six whole volumes containing nothing but thugs, all looking exactly alike?

O'Reilly reappeared as I flipped over the last page of volume six. He raised his eyebrows.

"None look even vaguely familiar," I said. "Look, Mr. O'Reilly, I have a business to run – and preferably not by long distance."

"No one even comes close? Are you sure?" O'Reilly could be frustratingly hard of hearing.

"Not even this close." I flattened my palms, tilted them sideways, and opened up a wide space between them as if I were some fisherman telling about the biggest one that ever got away.

"So sure, in fact, that in the beginning you didn't have a clue as to what the guy looked like. Now, you tell me you're dead sure none of these mug shots come close." He had trouble keeping the sarcasm in check, and it came through loud and clear. I didn't like his use of the word dead, either.

My mind's eye flashed a Mach-6 vision of blond hair carelessly tucked beneath a black stocking cap; a brown raincoat; a big gun. The picture was indefinably hazy.

"Something?" O'Reilly asked. He was very bright, this guy.

"Nothing." And yet...?

"Often things come back. You'll keep me posted." It wasn't a question.

I pushed back my chair and stood. O'Reilly didn't protest. "We appreciate your cooperation," he said instead.

"And where's Mr. Greenlyne? I assume you're questioning him as well."

"He'll be staying for awhile," as if Stan had just checked in at some swanky resort hotel. "Shall I call a cab, or have one of my men drive you?" All right, so the man could be civil when he wanted to be.

"A cab, thanks." I appreciated the theatricality of returning to work in a squad car, but I'd had enough drama for one day.

* * *

Betty greeted me, always ready to paint a pretty picture. "You look like shit!" she said.

"So ask me how far off the mark that is from how I feel."

She followed me into my office. "How far off the mark is that from how..."

"Right on the money! How'd the show go?"

"Everybody wanted to buy a Draqual while the gun was still smoking and the King of Ladies' Undies was locked in the slammer."

She followed me into the bathroom. "Betty, I can take a leak on my own."

She retreated, and I shut the door. First things first. I checked the mirror. Yuk! I pissed, washed my hands, splashed cold water on my face, and ran my damp fingers through a layered razor-cut that tumbled strands of hair to just the proper coif. I then rejoined Betty in my office, stripped off my jacket, and started unbuttoning my shirt.

"I would have thought you'd be too pooped for fun and games," she said.

I rewarded her with a smirk and headed for the armoire where I kept several fresh changes of clothes. The day had taken its toll.

Betty watched.

Although my naked chest was not what I would have preferred, had I been given a choice, some people – men and women, including Betty – seemed to find it sexy. Betty and I had almost gone to bed together way back when, but she'd finally thought better of it: "Too much baggage to take you and your manhood hang-ups into the same four-poster." Which hadn't made me very happy at the time. Especially since she was right – about the search for my manhood, that is. Which wouldn't have stopped me from firing her. My father, ever more wise with each passing year, had put his foot down: "You don't let someone go for getting it right." He had the final say, and I wasn't around the shop often enough to insist scoring a point while losing it anyway. By the time I had moved into the company fast track and was shedding inhibitions right and left during sessions with Dr. Melissa, I was able to look back with a somewhat more enlightened perspective. Betty had never held it against me.

"Yum, yum," she said. "Almost good enough to..."

"Please don't say 'eat'," I warned her, "lest you risk embarrassment by witnessing pronounced evidence of my raging lust."

She had a cute, arching left eyebrow and long sexy lashes. The latter she batted over deep-hazel eyes. Sometimes I got the impression that, if I tried again, I might be more successful in getting her to bed. Trouble is, I wasn't the stud, quite literally, I once was. Having gotten my head together enough to realize the motivation for my rampant promiscuity, my libido went into low gear, even more so since AIDS had come on the scene. I was definitely in love with my hand, raw liver, cantaloupe, and watermelon-in-season.

"Maybe, just maybe, you are now presentable enough to make a good impression on Mrs. Kaney," Betty said.

"Mrs. Greta Kaney?" I still wasn't exactly batting a hundred.

"She must have a lover," Betty continued. "She bought three sexy numbers and stayed for immediate fittings. You want to do some of your famous ass-kissing and tell her how pleased you are that she shopped Draqual?"

Did I?

Gerald Kaney's death was somehow connected to that of Don deZinn, and both murders were somehow intertwined with a gunman's unsuccessful assassination attempt of only just a few hours ago. Now, here was the ex-wife of a dead Gerald Kaney camped out on my doorstep the very same day I dodged a bullet, resisted a non-arrest, and had been told that I may be on a gangster's hit list. And that thought reminded me suddenly that I still must call Mildred Rollins for an appointment to see her husband: no longer just a matter of saving Stan Greenlyne's ass but mine as well. I was feeling pretty paranoid.

I did a quick deep-breather from the pit of my stomach. "I suppose seeing Mrs. Kaney can't hurt," I replied.

"I'll see if she's still here and buzz you."

I headed back to the washroom. I splashed some Guerlain from the pint bottle I kept for just such sweaty days. In a final, passing glance at the mirror, an image of the shooter appeared to me for one lingering instant.

I had, of course, flashed the very same image before. At the station house. There, not all of the gunman's features had jelled. This time, the image was longer-lasting and clearer. "I know you, you bastard!" When and where was available to me, too, if only I could...

The intercom sounded... and bam! I had it!

"She's in Cubicle B," Betty intruded on my thoughts.

I asked my secretary to dial the police. O'Reilly must have been sitting on his phone. I refused to let myself conjure up the picture usually associated with that worn cliché.

"Yes, Mr. Draqual?" he asked expectantly.

"About the man who shot at Stan and me..." I couldn't keep the excitement and pleasure out of my voice. I was like a kid who has been complimented on some amazing feat of daring-do. "I've seen him before," I continued. "Recently. On a street corner with a couple of working girls. One of the professionals is a regular Draqual customer."

"Great, Mr. Draqual! I appreciate your calling back so soon. Now, does this regular Draqual customer have a name?" soothing and coaxing as if I would fly from him at any moment.

"Paul Cortland."

Not even a slight pause. "Who works under the name of... Candie Kane? Lily White?"

"Nothing nearly so exotic. Try Paula."

"Wouldn't have an address for this Paul... sorry, Paula?"

I gave it to him... along with a phone number.

Chapter Five

Mildred was out. A Spanish-accented voice assured me Mrs. Rollins, when once back, would be sure to return my call.

At least, Greta Kaney was where I thought she'd be. She looked good in an oyster-grey silk slip bordered with hand-tatted lace which had been untimely, but very carefully, ripped from the bodice of a Seventeenth-century Irish wedding gown. The Costa del Sol had given Greta one of those exquisite tans which remained in fashion despite skin cancer scares.

"Mr. Draqual!? Thank-you again for allowing me to attend your showing." She paused as if considering the propriety of her next statement. "I would gather the gunfire business has been straightened out. Your lovely Miss Meiken was kind enough to tell me how awkward it was for you." I knew she didn't realize she sounded condescending, but it was annoying all the same.

Her no doubt surgically-lifted face conveyed concern. Her plucked-to-thin eyebrows slid toward a crease which formed at the bridge of her slightly retrousse nose. Her cupid's-bow mouth moued slightly beneath the palest of pale-pink lipstick.

"It's ongoing conjecture that the police are dealing with a disgruntled, bad-shot fan of Stan Greenlyne," I said. "You do know Stan Greenlyne, I believe."

Her lips lost their purse but stayed crunched at the corners. If I hadn't suspected she was incapable of admitting such sentiments, even if she possessed them, I would have sworn she was about ready to say: "'Tant pis!' Too bad they missed."

She knew Stan, of course. But I wanted confirmation. Gerald was involved with Stan in the work on the Don deZinn book, but whether that involvement had begun before, during, or after the divorce, I couldn't recall -- if I'd ever known.

"Gerald knew Stan. Gerald knew lots of people," she replied. She torqued on long legs and looked down over her no doubt surgically-firmed backside to check the hemline being adjusted by the kneeling fitter. When you had Greta's kind of legs, you didn't hide a fraction more than necessary, even beneath Draqualian silk and heirloom lace.

I didn't recognize the fitter. "I'll finish up here, Miss...?"

"Petersen. I'm subbing for Mr. Kaiser."

"Well, Miss Petersen... if Mrs. Kaney doesn't object..."

Mrs. Kaney did not object. "I'd be flattered by your personal attention," was the way she put it, like the Duchess to the Bishop.

I pirated Miss Petersen's wrist pincushion as she was on her way out the door, and I moved in for a closer look at Greta Kaney. On the way to a slow kneel, I was impressed by her bulgeless middle: there were no lines of an underlying support garment in evidence. Silk was sexy but unforgiving; forgiveness was something customers often mistakenly expected as a natural recompense for paying through the nose for self-indulgence.

"I believe you and Gerald saw each other regularly," Greta ventured.

I placed another pin. "Regularly?" Her inflection had indicated more than the reality. While Gerald and I had met for the occasional game of squash, it was more often a case of bumping into each other at some "in" place.

"'Saw the Lingerie King,' he'd say," she said. "'I'm always impressed by his exceptional good looks.'"

I didn't know what, exactly, she was getting at, but it sounded like a possible come-on.

I looked up – past a waterfall of grey silk and lace, past no doubt surgically-augmented breasts – to her no doubt beauty-parlor-augmented blonde hair cascading over tanned shoulders in a profusion of high-art hairdresser curls.

"Which I always found interesting in that you weren't Gerald's type at all," she continued, less coy now and increasingly bolder by the second.

"Oh?" as nonchalantly as I was able to manage after having been zonked in the psyche.

"You knew you weren't, I would imagine."

"The police asked. I told them Gerald was heterosexual."

She smiled. She had a nice smile over no doubt surgically-improved teeth. "Of course, I'll tell them the same. The truth is quite different, as you are no doubt aware."

"What if your ex-husband's killer is gay?"

"My ex-husband's killer is gangland," she stated. "Isn't that what Stan Greenlyne implied to you? He certainly insinuated as much to me. For the obvious reasons, I do not wish to point a finger at Clem Rollins."

"You've heard the tape?" I finished with the pins and

rose from my kneeling position.

"Have you heard it?" she wanted to know. Our conversation was quickly deteriorating into typical question-for-question psycho-babble.

"I wasn't Gerald's type, remember?"

"And Stan Greenlyne isn't your type," she said. Insinuating what? Whatever, I wasn't going to argue. If she believed I was gay, then let her believe it. My days of resorting to school-yard fisticuffs when called Sissy, by some adolescent bully, were over.

"That leaves Don deZinn," she continued. "Did Don deZinn ask you to act as liaison between Stan Greenlyne and him before he approached Gerald about working on the book?"

"No, actually." I leaned against a wall and folded my arms (Dr. Melissa called it my defensive posture), and I wondered where this conversation was going. "I had a new collection to get out when Stan's winning bid came through," I said.

"Gerald was delighted with the opportunity," she replied. "After he was promoted to Production Vice President of the network, he had very little real work to do. If they couldn't trust him in front of the cameras, how could they trust him in business matters?"

"He seldom came across as being all that drunk," I

replied.

"He was good at covering it. Which kept him on the air as long as he was. However, if you'd seen as much of him as I did, as much of him as the network executives did, you'd have spotted telltale signs immediately. No one, even Gerald, wanted the public to spot them, too. That's why he didn't make a fuss when he was taken off the air. He coveted the persona he had built over the years." She paused briefly and then backtracked. "I have no intention of telling O'Reilly anything gay-related. Gerald was an adequate husband, more adequate at the beginning, of course, than at the end. And it didn't make for a messy divorce, although it might well have ended up that way. Because, if there was the question of his sexuality, I wasn't exactly the naive, teary-eyed, neurotic and injured wife, who patiently awaited the mending of her erring husband's ways." So there!

Her other purchases – a gold teddy with matching peignoir and a light-pistachio camisole – had already been marked for alterations.

"But I'm keeping you from other customers," she decided.

Her small-talk was insightful and fascinating, but I wasn't sure how much more I wanted to hear. I'd called Mildred Rollins for a meeting with her husband, and I didn't want to carry into that conversation any burden of information with which Greta Kaney might inadvertently shackle me. Clem would know genuine innocence when he saw it.

"I would very much like to have you over for supper tomorrow night... if you're free, naturally," she surprised. (I could hear Dr. Melissa in the background: "If you genuinely weren't out to play Sam Spade, you could easily have made excuses"). "I'm staying at the Plenden's while Carla and Ron are in Italy," she continued. "Carla tells me you and she are old friends. About eight o'clock, then? I'm a very good cook, and I understand you're an attentive eater."

She stepped from the fitter's platform and entered the small dressing salon where her street clothes would have been carefully placed on a rack in one corner. She would then cross her arms over her breasts, deepening her cleavage, and grasp the hemline of the slip with long delicate fingers. Her arms would then move slowly upward, peeling rippling grey silk and lace from her pampered body. Her bare breasts are symmetrical and firm. She throws back her shoulders and aims her large nipples toward her own reflection in the floor-to-ceiling mirror. Admiring her own nakedness, she runs her hands over her body before reaching for her blouse...

Greta emerged from the salon fully clothed. I had a hard-on – not from passion but from automatic conditioning, whenever any acceptable-by-society stimulus presented itself. Like Pavlov's dog, I slobbered whenever the bell tinkled, regardless of whether hungry or not.

I didn't shift or try to conceal the bulge at my crotch. (The first time this had happened at a fitting, I'd been embarrassed and had tried to make my erection less obvious. I'd since learned that most women are flattered).

"Apropos my remark about not being a teary-eyed, stay-at-home wife, Stud... I may call you Stud, mayn't I? Well, when I married Gerald, I wasn't exactly a babe in the woods. But I didn't know everything there was to know about how people lived out their sex lives, either." She nodded toward my erection-delineated crotch. "Gerald could do that, too," she continued. "In the beginning, I mistakenly believed any such necromancer would be all man. Not that what I found out later about him made him any less a man, whatever the definition of manhood is these days. It's just that I'd always expected my competition to be other attractive women."

* * *

By the close of the day, I still hadn't received a return call from Mildred Rollins and decided I'd try her again later in the afternoon from my apartment.

I had just thrown on my jacket and was going out the door when Betty put through a call directly from Clem Rollins. He was gracious and apologetic. He wanted to know if I could meet with him early the next morning at his home out on Long Island. He'd send a car. I said "Yes, of course," and gave him the address of my apartment building. I was dead certain he hadn't summoned me to talk about ladies' underwear, but I was too curious about the man to be overly anxious As my sainted grandmother used to say to me: "Stud, curiosity killed you-know-what!" But being the smart-ass I was, even then, I always replied: "Yeah, grandma. But satisfaction brought it back!" With Clem Rollins, I was willing to gamble either way.

Chapter Six

The Ford Pinto was driven by a trendily-dressed young man who introduced himself as "Buddy". I saw him as too clean-cut to be a hoodlum, but that was a self-delusionary ploy to ease the tension I'd built up overnight rehearsing over and over in my mind how I was going to handle the interview with Clem Rollins. Somehow, I had to convince Clem that I knew nothing from nothing about what Don deZinn might have put on a goddamn tape.

"Coffee in the brown thermos, tea in the green," Buddy said. He held the door and ushered me into the backseat where two containers were kept upright in a narrow cardboard box lodged against the opposite door. "Help yourself to whichever – whenever."

He hopped in behind the wheel and activated all door locks from a switch on the dash. The sound of the simultaneous clicks pulled me out of my complacency. All exits from the car had been effectively sealed, and I was, for all intents and purposes, imprisoned in a Pinto.

"Morning paper," Buddy said, tossing it over the front seat. "Richy Biglow missing. Know him?" He adjusted the rearview mirror so we could eyeball each other.

All I'd focused on in that morning's paper had been a medium-sized boldface lead-in headline: "KING OF SILK SLIPS GUNMAN". The relatively short news item was accompanied by a photo snapped of me at an AIDS benefit I'd attended the year before.

Richy had been a regular on the talk shows back when Johnny Carson was king of late-night TV. Richy's forte was mimicking celebrities, and his impersonation of Carson, with salacious references to Johnny's wives, numbers six through whatever, had gotten Richy blackballed from the networks. I had heard, via the grapevine, that he still managed regular appearances in Vegas.

But I wasn't interested in Richy Biglow. Or in tea. Or in coffee. All I wanted was to get the conversation I was about to have with Clem Rollins exactly right. Ordinarily, I might have suspected a move on my company. Clem's tentacular influence was well-entrenched throughout the garment industry. Had he really wanted a piece of my action, there was not much I could have done. More than one business had been ruined in futile attempts to avoid the inevitable. If I couldn't persuade Clem Rollins I knew next to nothing about what Don deZinn might have taped, which could incriminate Clem, there's no doubt I'd become just one more large chunk of fish-food at the bottom of the East River.

Clem lived in a typically middle-American suburb. There were no acres of landscaped lawn, no gates, no gate house, no guards, no access drive, no body searches, and no metal detectors – that I could see. The house was surrounded by a picket fence which enclosed a neat but small front patch of tulip-bordered lawn. A cobblestone walk led from the garage to the front door. Clem Rollins, still in robe, slippers, and pajamas, came out along the walkway to meet me. He was in his seventies and hadn't aged well. His face was a mass of wrinkles and loose flesh, his body thin and wasted. Spindly forearms and bony, veined hands poked out from the sleeves of his robe.

"Thank-you for coming all the way out here, my boy." His handshake was firm. He placed his left hand in the small of my back and propelled me toward the front door where Mildred met us in welcome. She was neatly groomed and wore a floral housedress with functional black shoes.

"Mr. Draqual, how nice!" she said.

Mildred had always been friendly and warm toward me. Even motherly. It was only when she put on a piece of Draqualian lingerie that I had a glimpse of her utter attractiveness. A low-cut bit of expensively draped silk made her years fall away and caused her body to shift itself into tighter, more shapely groupings, as if she'd been awarded the gift of a rejuvenating elixir.

"I'll get some coffee and let you men talk," she continued. She motioned me into a chintz-covered couch; her husband sank into a well-worn wing-back chair.

Mildred was no sooner through the door than she was back again with a tray laden with coffee pot, cookies, and two cups and saucers.

"If you need anything, just give me a call." A parting kindness which was so typical of her. Nothing in my present surroundings, or in Mildred's manner, suggested that she regularly plopped down four-figure sums for items of silk which, more often than not, could be stuffed, with room to spare, into the well of a thimble.

Clem poured coffee with a slight tremor which rattled the china.

"My wife likes you," he said. "She says you're a nice man. She thinks you're very handsome, too." He eyed me over the rim of his cup. "I agree."

I read nothing in his eyes, but his smile wasn't quite

warm enough to stop the chills cascading the length of my spine. I drank my coffee and welcomed its mouth-burning heat. I'd been told before that I was good-looking, but being told by Clem Rollins, of all people, left me uneasy. I wasn't exactly terrified. Just speechless.

"Do you think my saying that makes me queer?" he asked.

"I think...," and here I inserted the name of a popular movies star, "...is exceptionally good-looking." I waited for him to make the mistake so many others had made; namely, "Stud, I already know you're queer."

Clem surprised me. "Exactly my point," he said. "I think you're good-looking. I'm not queer. You think what's-his-name is good-looking. You're not queer." His smile became warmer and more genuine. "I've checked. Granted, you've been in a few group sessions where you were bound to have laid a hand on a hard dick or two, but I can't find any man who's ever slept with you one-to-one. A lot of them wished they had, even blatantly say they have, but none of that checks out under my kind of scrutiny."

He had another sip of coffee and leaned back into the shadowy depths of his wing chair.

"Does it bother you that people – some, not all, mind you – find you too handsome to be straight?" he asked.

"It used to bother me a good deal," I replied. The conversation was taking a turn I would never have expected in a thousand years: philosophical almost, and certainly amateurishly psychological.

"Your shrink must have made you realize how some people feel uncomfortable by anyone they think is too perfect... in looks, say, or intelligence, or anything else for that matter. They're never happy until they've ferreted out some flaw. But from my point of view, what two consenting adults do in the privacy of their own bedroom is nobody else's goddamn business. Not that I've always been so liberal, but times change."

He leaned toward me again, poured himself a fresh cup of coffee, and invited me to a refill with a slight incline of his head.

"But I don't have a shrink," he said as he settled back into his chair once more. "I can't afford one."

I was certain he was now headed in yet another, and entirely new, direction. Surely being unable to afford a shrink had nothing to do with his bank account.

"So," he said after another sip of coffee, "my head isn't as straight as yours." He paused briefly. "I read in the paper about Stan Greenlyne and your altercation, outside your office building, with a man and his gun." He paused again. "You and Stan survived, I'm pleased to see."

"Yes."

"And you two then went to lunch."

"Yes."

Then, he gave me the opportunity I'd been waiting for. "Did Stan mention me?"

"What he wanted was to persuade me to arrange a meeting between you and him," I jumped in.

"Oh? Why you as go-between?"

I shrugged. "I know him. I know your wife. She knows you."

"Stan say why he wants this meeting? Why he couldn't arrange it himself by simply calling my secretary?"

"He thinks he has something you might want. He'd prefer handing it over, no questions asked, with as few people involved in the transaction as possible."

"For a price?"

"No. He was quite specific about that."

"He say what he wants to give me?"

"A tape."

"Which came to him through Don deZinn, via Gerald Kaney?"

"He mentioned that, yes."

"Saying I was gay?"

There was absolutely nothing I could comfortably say in response to that, so I didn't even try.

Clem airily waved a hand in absolution. "You mustn't think I'm coming down heavily on you because of whatever Stan Greenlyne may or may not have done or said. You know the cops are following him around, afraid I'm out to get him by hiring some nincompoop delinquent to shoot him down in the streets, for Christ's sake!" He shook his head in disbelief that anyone would think him so stupid, and I tried to appear equally disbelieving. "Tell me more about this tape," he continued.

"Part of Don deZinn's autobiography, the early years."

"Linking me to Don. Sexually?"

"Just 'linking', is all Stan said."

"Don and I were linked. Sex, but not sexual." He paused and squinted as if appraising my intelligence. "Does that make any sense to you?"

I truly did not understand what he was getting at, but I didn't have the balls to admit it, or to ask him for clarification.

"I sometimes called on Don for services," he continued. "For friends. For friends of friends. For enemies. For friends of enemies. I won't bore you with details." I nodded assent. "It was a long time ago. Too long ago to be of any consequence, or of any threat, now, to this old man. Which leads to a couple of conclusions. One, either Don lied to make his story juicier – although, for the life of me, I can't understand why he would need any embellishment. Or two, Stan Greenlyne is fibbing for reasons of his own. Can you help me with this, Mr. Draqual?"

"I don't think I can, Mr. Rollins, and it's not because I wouldn't like to. I simply just don't know anything more."

Clem seemed to accept this, to my utter amazement.

"Stan being baby-sat by the cops makes a meeting between us... difficult, shall we say. When you see him, you might tell him that, and ask him to get back to me... through you."

So that was the hook!

"Yes, of course. I'll do that."

Clem then gave me a lecherous grin. "My wife adores you and likes your stuff. She has one of your more scanty red items that she sometimes wears, and which I find particularly..." He leaned forward and placed his cup and saucer gently on the tray between us. "I needn't say more."

Mildred appeared, through the connecting door, as if by magic, just as if she'd been listening and wanted to nip this conversation in the bud, right now! "More coffee?" she asked.

"No thank-you, my dear. Mr. Draqual is just leaving."

I stood and placed my cup on the tray beside Clem's.

"So soon?" Mildred sounded genuinely disappointed.

I wanted out of there, no question, and I wanted to shove a fist down Stan Greenlyne's fat throat for conning me into this visit in the first place. "Afraid so, Mrs. Rollins," I replied. "I'm hoping to see you in the City soon, though. I've something in red..."

"Ah, my favorite, red!" interjected Clem.

"...that you may like."

"Really? How nice of you to mention it!" She seemed, literally, to beam.

No guarantees, of course, but I think it's definitely you."

"There goes the bank account!" bemoaned Clem, surprisingly and suddenly spry and playful. He looked in Mildred's direction with genuine affection, winked at her, and waved me good-bye. Mildred saw me out.

* * *

On the way back to the City, Buddy took what I knew to be a wrong turn. "Shortcut," he said when I called him on it.

I wasn't up to shortcuts. Clem Rollins was out to silence Stan Greenlyne for something Clem thought I knew. Dead people don't talk. Don didn't. Gerald didn't. Stan and I wouldn't.

I broke into another cold sweat, and I was suddenly reminded that I shouldn't have had that much of Mildred's delicious coffee.

Chapter Seven

If it had not been for a car which spun out of control on the freeway, broadsided by the one following it, and then smashed by another headed from the opposite direction, our route would have been via the shortcut Buddy said would lop about ten miles off our trip. I checked the mileage on a map as soon as I was safely and happily back in my office.

I called Stan and told him that Clem agreed to a meeting, provided there were no cops around. Stan said he'd get back to me. I had a feeling he was going to chicken out.

Which left me to contemplate my date with Greta Kaney. If this was a little game she'd thought up, in which the primary rule of play was fuck me to prove you're not queer, then I wasn't interested. I was just about to call her to cancel out when Betty put her through on line one.

"Hello, Stud," said Greta. "I'm sorry to bother you. But would you mind terribly if we ate out? Frankly, I'm running late and just don't have the time to come up with the kind of home-cooked meal I promised."

"Would you prefer we postpone until a later date when it's more convenient for you?" I asked. I honestly hoped she'd take me up on this suggestion straight away. But naturally, she picked my weak spot and played on my guilt.

"I was rather looking forward to our evening. Of course, if you'd really prefer..."

Greta in a restaurant I could handle. Nightcaps in the Plenden's brownstone I wasn't so sure about. So, I opted for what was safer. "Eight o'clock, then," I replied.

"At the Villa d'Este on Sixty-second, between Madison and Park... if that's all right with you. The food's good."

Cocktails at the Villa d'Este I could handle.

My mating dance had slowed from a wild disco beat to a stately pavane since onset of therapy. Dr. Melissa would say – and did – that I was still playing detective. But finding out that Gerald had been bisexual piqued my curiosity, and Greta could be pumped in a public place without my running the risk of too much intimacy.

"I may be a few minutes late," she said. "Be sure to

wait. As you know, getting a cab that time of the evening can be horrid."

I promised to be patient, hung up, and returned to some business which had been solely neglected during the past two days. Betty provided the next jolt.

"You know my sister who nurses at St. Luke's?" I put design sketches to one side. Betty seemed anxious enough for me to expect something not nice.

"Gee, Betty, I hope there's nothing wrong in your family."

"No, no! It's nothing like that. But Jenny called to tell me that Paul Cortland has just been admitted into ER. The scuttlebutt is: police brutality."

"O'Reilly, you asshole bastard!" I rasped.

"Are you thinking what I am?" Betty asked. Her sister knew Paul/Paula from the AIDS ward. Paul had been tested HIV-negative, but several of his friends – of mine, and of Betty's, and of almost everyone else I knew – hadn't been so lucky.

"What is you're thinking?" I replied.

"That Paul's asking for you, because someone told him we gave his name and address to a queen-hating dickhead." Betty's language was strong, and it mirrored the emotion she showed.

"O'Reilly, you asshole!" I repeated.

"You going to the hospital?"

"I'm going."

"I'll call a cab."

O'Reilly intercepted me in the hospital lobby. He was genuinely apologetic but defensive. "How was I to know the officer assigned to the interview with Paul had a nephew who'd been denutted by a demented street hustler?"

"I hope Paul slaps the police and the City with the thoroughest lawsuit you've ever had the privilege of weaseling out of."

"He didn't exactly help matters by being uncooperative and disrespectful," O'Reilly replied.

"That sounds like a very good excuse for putting him in the hospital," I said facetiously. "It might do you some good to remember that to get respect, you gotta give it."

O'Reilly counterattacked, but I didn't hear. Not because I wasn't interested. Reporters had spotted me and made a rush. The shooting had made me fairly worthy news copy, and my appearance at the hospital caused a feeding frenzy which had somehow escaped me until then. I suppose I have O'Reilly and his minions to thank for the quick action and fast interference which enabled me to escape with all limbs in one piece.

What I said, by way of thanks, was: "Where's Paul?"

"We'll take the service elevator," O'Reilly answered.

"Don't expect to sit in on the conversation, or have any of your men-in-blue there, either. Give me static, and I'll call my lawyer to ride your ass."

"Listen, Mr. Draqual, I couldn't do the interview with Cortland myself. I was too busy with an anonymous source who would only pass some key information on Richy Biglow to me."

"Fuck you! Fuck your source! Fuck your homophobic associate! And fuck Richy Biglow who's probably missing only because he hopes press coverage will resurrect what's left of a career which has long since been flushed down the toilet." I was on a roll.

Police violence made me angry, to say the very least, particularly police brutality against gays. I'd been accused of being queer so often that I'd developed an empathy with most fags. And I hated myself for probably being halfway responsible for some slap-happy cop winding up on Paul Cortland's doorstep.

Jenny Meiken met us in the corridor outside the ER and separated me from O'Reilly with the same skillfulness O'Reilly had used in steering me clear of the reporters. Jenny was younger than Betty and not as pretty, but that hadn't kept her from a good-looking husband, two great kids, and a successful nursing career.

"How's Paul?" I asked her.

"Looking far worse than he actually is. I snapped a few pictures while he's looking his worst." She patted her uniform pocket.

"His lawyer here?"

"Been here for the past two weeks. Fourth floor." The AIDS ward. "Critical."

"Jesus!"

"Paul's at a loss. We figured that since the cop laid this all on your doorstep..."

"Unfortunately true," I said. "It was supposed to have been a routine question-and-answer. Paul might know the person who took a shot at Stan Greenlyne and me outside my building."

"Why shooting at you, by the way?"

"Why shooting at Stan Greenlyne is probably more like it."

"Being a nurse and all, I hate to say it, but Stan Greenlyne deserves... well, a little rough treatment. He's a slime bag."

"Hopefully without me in the crossfire," I replied.

"Amen to that!"

Jenny was talking pretty rough, too, I noticed, but probably with good reason. Telaman Press' NURSIE had blasted Jenny's chosen profession as it was practiced by the slovenly and homicidal staff of a fictitious Jefferson Davis Memorial Hospital. The book had managed to zap not only the entire nursing profession but, also, the President of the former Confederacy and every state south of the Mason-Dixon. It was one of Stan's masterpieces of vituperation.

Jenny steered me through a door on our left. She was right: Paul looked bad. Split lower and upper lip, each in two places. One black eye, the other coloring. A long scratch along his left cheek. Nasty contusions and abrasions on his cheekbones.

"You came!" He obviously had not been as confident as Jenny and O'Reilly that I would show up.

"Damned right!" My relationship with Paul, until now, had been mainly business, although I had run into him at an occasional AIDS-related fund-raiser where drag, albeit grudgingly, was accepted. Normally, I wouldn't have come running to his bedside; normally, my name wouldn't have been the first off the lips of a patient in the Emergency Room of St. Luke's Hospital.

"Jesus, I'm sorry about all of this, Paul." There was a telephone on the tall taboret beside his bed, and I reached for it.

"Dial nine for outside," Jenny said.

"I kept telling the cop I hadn't seen Jack or Glennis in

over a week," Paul said. "Even then, it had been only in passing, on a street corner. The jack-off kept insisting I was lying." It was hard to decipher what came through Paul's blood-encrusted lips, bracketed as they were by his bruised and battered face.

"Guy they're looking for is named Jack, then? Or Glennis?" I asked.

"Jack Fornal," Paul mumbled. "Two-legged piece of shit. Don't know what Glennis sees in him. Treats her like his personal punching bag."

"Glennis have a last name?"

"Rhynne."

"Not Glen Rhynne?"

"Naw. Jack would freak out with anything but a real woman."

I reached Marty on the line, and he said he'd be right down. This made me happy. He was finally earning the sizable retainers I'd been paying him for the past several years.

"Don't talk to anyone until my lawyer shows," I told Paul.

I turned to Jenny. "Any problems barricading the press?"

"We get high-profile people in here all the time. We've got the routine down pat."

"Marty will know how much cop-blame to spoon-feed the media and when to schedule feeding time."

Paul looked relieved, though in his condition, it was hard to tell what he was thinking. "I really don't know where Jack or Glennis is," he repeated. One of the splits in his lower lip started to bleed.

"Not your fault the cop wasn't listening."

"Sadistic pig!" Jenny concluded.

I didn't know whether it would help or hurt to mention that the cop responsible was acting out frustrations caused by a nephew's castration. I did know that I didn't want to make excuses for myself. Excuses could not possibly compensate for any of this.

I checked my watch. A nervous reflex born of having done all I'd come to do, said all I'd come to say, and having made all the gestures I'd come to make, in order to salve my guilty conscience. All that was left was a bedside vigil, holding Paul's hand: a role to which neither he nor I found me particularly well-suited.

"You want your exit cluttered with press?" Jenny asked. "Or do you want clear sailing?"

Marty would want me to leave any statements up to him. "Your sister ran interference to keep them off my back, after the shooting, but even she'd be hard-pressed here."

"How about just one reporter?" Jenny suggested. "Kim Toole thinks he's found the one and only secret exit to this place. We only need to act surprised when he jumps out with microphone in hand."

Toole wasn't my first choice; someone from the gay press would have been better, but he'd do in a pinch, and this was a pinch. If caught on the run, I could say what I had to say and leave Marty to damage control.

I became Theseus in a Hippocratic labyrinth, Jenny my Ariadne. We encountered Toole at a fire exit.

"This anything to do with the shooting, Mr. Draqual?" Toole was a loner, was freelance, was print media, so there were no klieg lights. He was a short man who relied on charm, not obnoxiousness, to get a story. I didn't recall him being either pro- or anti-gay. If the latter, he wouldn't likely have gotten Jenny's go-ahead.

I stopped and took several deep breaths. I wanted the playback from Toole's tape recorder to be clear and concise.

"There is something desperately wrong with a city's police department when respectable, tax-paying citizens can be shot at on a busy downtown street, in broad daylight, the cops more interested in brutally beating up a source of information on that shooting, because of his sexual orientation, than in apprehending whomever fired the gun!"

I wasn't outing Paul. He'd "done rag" publicly for years. A couple of years ago, when he'd crashed a high-society Christmas ball, wearing a black Draqualian-silk peignoir, he'd made "People" magazine and received a silk teddy free-of-charge from a grateful and appreciative Draqual Fashions, Inc.

"An information source, in what respect?" asked Toole.

"Talk to Inspector O'Reilly. He's in charge of the investigation, and he's the officer who assigned the sadistic cop who 'interviewed' Paul Cortland."

Jenny expertly stepped between us, and I made my move behind her. Through the door. Across the alley. Into the back room of a surgical supply store where a stock man, who had been forewarned, was waiting. He led me out the front door of the shop to a waiting cab at the curb. I cell-phoned Betty to tell her I hoped she could carry through the rest of the day without me. Betty assured me she'd give it her best try. Then, I gave the driver my apartment address.

It was only after I'd closed and locked the double doors to my apartment, with a sigh of great relief, that I realized I wasn't quite alone – or all that safe – within the shadowy confines of my own entranceway.

Chapter Eight

"How the hell did you get in here?"

Stan stepped forward into the light.

"UNSAFE BEHIND LOCKED DOORS by Cleveland Moore," he said. Moore was a locksmith and serial killer. Before the cops nabbed him, and before Telaman Press signed a ghost writer to provide his supposedly first-person account, he'd molested thirteen women and had left nine of them headless in their uptown Manhattan apartments.

"I'm calling the police!" I was pissed off with Stan to begin with, and I certainly didn't want him invading my space. "Speaking of the police..." I wasn't sure whether he'd gotten the protection he'd asked for; although, Clem Rollins had told me he had. "Where are they? Aiding and abetting a breaking-and-entering?"

"I slipped my tail. Not too difficult once I pinned down his MO."

I tried to recall the name of yet another Telaman Press best-seller which had been written by a cop who revealed mammoth police-department corruption while detailing all the intricacies of surveillance technique. "Isn't the whole point of police protection to have cops handy?"

"I need cops?" Stan replied. He upturned lily-white palms. "I thought Clem had agreed to a meeting."

"He did." I led Stan through the hallway and into the living room. Since he was here anyway, and since there was no way I could think of to get rid of him, I might as well find out why. I needed a drink. I poured a scotch without offering hospitality and poured myself a second before I spotted the small packet on my coffee table. "Santa Claus bearing gifts while I was away?"

"A little surprise," Stan answered. "Would have been more of one if you hadn't shown up unexpectedly. What brings you home early?"

"That's none of your goddamn business, Stan." I walked to the coffee table, hefted the envelope, and without even reading the note left beneath it, I knew what it was. "No way, Stan!"

"Come on, Stud." His voice was smooth as the silk with which I sheathed rich women's naked bodies. "Where's the problem?"

"You asked for a meeting. Against my better

judgment, I smoothed the way. My job description does not include acting as courier for a ticking time bomb. I'd prefer that Clem never knew I was within a mile of this thing." It was the incriminating tape. Of course it was.

"I know I asked for the meet, but now I'm not really all that comfortable with the idea. It leaves me vulnerable. I'm just trying to be a good guy, and Clem might take advantage."

"So, set the guidelines to protect your ass. Ask him to meet you in a public place."

"Can't get more public than outside your building at high noon," Stan reminded. "Did that make for fair play?"

"This is your problem, Stan." I dropped the packet on the coffee table toward him. I did my Pontius Pilate routine by dusting my hands together several times.

"Maybe if you explained to me how this is worse for your health than the other way," he said. He sat on my couch; I could hear the protesting groans of underlying cushion, springs, and support structure.

"Get real, Greenlyne! You hand me the incriminating tape. I pass it to Clem Rollins. He wonders what I did with it in the interim. Played it for my own edification and amusement, maybe?"

"He knows you have the willpower to resist. I know

you do, too."

"Bullshit! The only thing Clem Rollins knows is that I sell his wife expensive lingerie. I'd never even met the man until I did you the favor you conned me into. Now, you want to impose even more upon my good nature."

"But Clem already suspects that Don told you everything," Stan replied.

"Does he? He didn't say so to me. He didn't hire a hit man to shoot me, either."

"I've come to think the gunman might have been out for both of us."

"That's the story most advantageous to you now, is it?"

"Clem wants to kill me for what he thinks I know about Don deZinn and him. He figures you know the same stuff, because you and Don were friends. Hell, even I figure Don told you everything. So, what if the jerk gunman was out to silence not only you, not only me, but the both of us?"

"I don't need this!"

"None of that ever crossed your mind?" Stan asked.

"Do you really think I would have naively let you take me to lunch if it had?"

"If you wanted to act innocent," Stan replied. "No one has ever said you aren't clever at masquerading as something you're not. I don't have to tell you how many people think you, your dick, and your ass, are up to guy sex every night."

That was it! "I want you out of here, now! Take your little time bomb with you. Now!"

"What would happen, I wonder, if I just left it with you? In spite of your protests?"

"As soon as you are out the door, I'll destroy it, pretend I've never seen it, and swear that you were never within fifty miles of this apartment. What's Clem to think when you don't provide him with the tape you've promised?"

"Kill me; you'd be responsible."

"Maybe I could live with that!"

"Could you?"

"Want to put me to the test?"

"Okay." Which didn't register until he was up and had moved away from me with the speed of a comet slingshot around some distant sun. His athletic dexterity and swiftness continued to amaze me.

"I'm not kidding, Stan!" I called after him.

"We'll see." He was already out the door.

I picked up the packet, fumbled the thing to the floor, retrieved it, and headed after him. The hallway was empty. I tried to reach the elevator before it closed. I didn't make it. I thought of the stairs and calculated the odds of beating the elevator thirty floors to the lobby. They were not in my favor.

"Bastard!"

I returned to my apartment determined to remove the cassette from its wrapper, smash it into little pieces with the hammer in my tool drawer, and heave the remains down the incinerator. Stan would sure as hell take my threats a little more seriously next time. If there was a next time. If Stan wasn't killed by some hood on the street, police protection to the contrary. Hell, presidents were assassinated in spite of an entire government agency geared to protect them. Neither Stan nor I was stupid enough to believe that a few cops would make any difference if Clem Rollins wanted either of us dead.

Stan didn't know me nearly well enough to believe I'd fall in with his plan. In fact, I didn't even know myself what I'd do now. If I hadn't yet smashed the tape to smithereens, that didn't mean I wouldn't do so as soon as I collected my wits and had another drink.

I called Stan's office. I knew he wouldn't have arrived there, already, but I wanted to charm his secretary into telling me where I could reach him, confront him, and stuff his goddamned tape down his blubber-insulated gullet.

"I am sorry, Mr. Draqual. Mr. Greenlyne isn't available at all today. Mr. Crisborne is in Switzerland, but I could transfer you through to Mr. Jonison."

"This is personal and genuinely important. Didn't Mr. Greenlyne leave an emergency number?"

"I'm sorry, but he didn't."

I called O'Reilly. I was feeling vicious and frustrated, and I wanted to gloat over police incompetence as much as wanting to find Stan.

"Inspector O'Reilly, it's important I talk with Stan Greenlyne right away. His office doesn't know where he is, but since you have him under surveillance, I was wondering if..."

O'Reilly interrupted me. "Police policy doesn't allow me to reveal his present whereabouts."

Police policy, my ass! But there was no sense in rubbing it in, or in telling him more than he knew already. And no point in having him wonder what the missing Stan had been up to in my apartment when he'd not been scheduled to be there.

"Thank-you, Inspector. And if you or one of your men happen to run into him...," I said and hung up.

I threw the cassette into my wall safe – to hell with any damage. "Sorry, Stan, but the tape was accidentally broken beyond repair," I could say. "I told you not to leave it. No way am I to blame for that bullet hole between your eyes."

I took a shower and jacked off. The latter not because of anything particularly stimulating that had happened during the day, but because I felt I needed a protective measure against the feminine wiles of Greta Kaney, to which I would shortly again be subjected. I'd so long lived to fuck any woman that my body still went into automatic countdown whenever I even thought of sex with one. Even though we were to meet in public, with no plans for private drinks, either before or after dinner, I didn't want to risk the vaguest chance of a spontaneous boner misrepresenting my intentions. And besides, even in the good old days, I'd been told there was more pleasure to be had from a vibrator up a cunt than from my hard-on mechanically and relentlessly pumping sweet pussy; I was saving her from discovery of that.

I tried to nap but couldn't. I kept examining options for disposition of the tape, none of which I really cared for. I fucked my hand a second time (no one has ever accused me of lacking endurance, or of not being up to whatever the occasion); rinsed myself under another, albeit quicker, shower; dressed and had another drink. I put on hold any final decision I might make about the tape.

Chapter Nine

I wasn't a regular at the Villa d'Este. Ma Collini's was closer, less expensive and satisfied my occasional craving for fettuccine Alfredo. The Villa d'Este maitre d' was a different man from the last time I'd eaten there, and he didn't recognize me.

"Mrs. Kaney's table?" I provided my own entree.

"Mr. Draqual? Of course, Mr. Draqual!" It was a nice touch, possibly just good enough to coax me back. "Mrs. Kaney is expecting you."

I was still in the vestibule when Giuseppe d'Este himself approached me through the length of his restaurant. This was VIP treatment indeed.

"Mr. Draqual! Long time no see." Giuseppe was another of the City's large men, a walking advertisement for the top-quality food of his four-star chef. We'd been introduced by the Maxwells, a few months ago, when I was their dinner guest, and I was flattered that Giuseppe remembered me; or, more likely, pretended to remember. "Mrs. Kaney she already here." He sounded as if he were straight off the boat, but that was strictly for atmosphere. He had been graduated from the Cordon Bleu School, Paris, and spoke aristocratic Florentine Italian, Oxcam English (when he wished), and Sixteenth Arrondissement French. He snapped up an oversized menu and led me down a short corridor to a small back annex reserved for special patrons.

Greta was dressed in an expensive spaghetti-strap frock which highlighted her tan. She smiled at me over a tulip glass poised at her high-gloss lips. A bottle of Dom Perignon nested in its bucket.

I cuffed a sleeve and looked at my watch. "I hope I'm not late," I said in greeting.

"I'm early," she replied.

Giuseppe pulled out my chair, settled me in, and poured champagne. "You wanna anything, letta Giuseppe know, huh?"

"Grazie tant, Joe," Greta said, smiling at his ludicrous accent. Giuseppe was delighted. His old-world bow was less graceful than one the equally fat Stan Greenlyne could have managed, but courtly just the same.

I looked around the small room. "I'm impressed," I said. "I doubt seriously if we'd gotten a table back here if I'd booked us in."

"Giuseppe owes me," she said, then paused. "For not naming him as a correspondent in my divorce."

This lady was full of surprises.

My mouth dropped open. "Giuseppe d'Este and Gerald!?" Giuseppe's wife sometimes table-hopped, chatting up the clientele. There were at least nine kids. One worked in the Mayor's office.

"I wouldn't normally have said anything about it," she added, "but I've purposely had enough drinks to gather courage to get rid of a lot of excess baggage I've been carrying around. Stud, I hope you don't mind my having chosen you as a sounding board?"

I couldn't answer that, not yet. My barely perceptible head shake indicated I didn't want to know any more about her and Gerald's life than was good for my health. I hinted as much. "Your ex-husband and I weren't really that close, you know."

"Oh, I originally thought I wanted to talk with someone who knew Gerald better than I. Not all that unusual, wouldn't you say: for a wife not really to know her husband, or a least to feel as if she didn't? But now, I just want a friendly ear to help me put it all into perspective." She ran her fingers through gilt-gold hair. "When I was in Europe," she went on, "I thought I missed this City. Now, I'm not so sure. Maybe it's because Gerald's murder dredges up too many cobwebs hidden in too many dark corners. There's something to be said for the sunlit, easy-going life-style of the Spanish Mediterranean."

I didn't bother with the menu. I sipped champagne and remained silent.

"Gerald hated Spain," she continued. "He took me there once for a week's holiday. He'd expected something quite different, and he complained constantly. We fought about it. This is a nasty thing to say, but my feeling was – and Gerald all but confirmed it – that he would have preferred Tonga." Tonga's king and queen, both enormously obese, had visited Washington only recently. "By then, of course, I knew Gerald's sexual preferences. It would have been kinder of me to pretend otherwise. He so prided himself on his all-American image. My having found out that he was a homosexual... what do you call it? chubby-chaser? – a disgusting expression! – made me irritable and defensive, which is quite understandable. I left the marriage less kindly than I went into it. And that pitiful mess with Ken Salmoth left a bitter taste in my mouth that's there to this day."

By this time, I was more or less reeling under the spate of her revelations and confidences. I endeavored to stay calm. "Ken Salmoth, the stockbroker?" I asked.

"Yes."

"Gerald and he were involved in some way?"

"I was with Gerald at the Four Seasons when he spotted Ken for the first time. You can't believe the change that came over him. It was a physical thing, very obvious. His eyes became brighter and his breathing quickened noticeably. Absolutely amazing! He was literally drooling – another awful word!" She smiled deprecatingly. "Well... perhaps drooling is a slight exaggeration."

"There were some rumors," I admitted. "The police dropped some hints, but nothing ever came of them as far as I know."

"When you say 'police', you mean 'O'Reilly', don't you?"

"You saw him this morning?"

"A man who's been around too long. Seen too much. He's close to burnout, and when it comes, it won't be a pretty picture."

"He asked you about Gerald and Salmoth?"

"Yes, and I acted surprised. Gerald gay? Never! Bisexual? Oh, maybe a few parties where gender made less and less difference as the evening wore on. You know the kind. But Gerald gay? Bi?" She laughed, but it was not a successful substitute for the real thing.

A waiter headed toward our table, but Greta nodded him away with the consummate skill of a buyer at auction seeking anonymity in a roomful of bidder-sharks.

"It always surprised me there were no more rumors than there were," she continued. "Gerald didn't seem all that discreet, at least to me. But then, that was the first time I'd seen him absolutely sexually enthralled. He set his cap (to use an old-fashioned phrase) for Ken, and got him. No matter what Ken might have wanted. Poor Ken."

"Takes two to tango: another old-fashioned phrase," I reminded her. Gerald had never done anything to make me dislike him.

"Ken didn't have a chance. Bowled over. Rolled over. And... well, you know." She wasn't accepting my argument that Ken's consent to his own seduction might just have been implicit, if not downright consensual. "I take it you didn't know him."

"Only what I read in the papers."

"Distortion. The truth wouldn't have been nearly as interesting. Ken was a boring man. It made much better copy to hint that he was one of the Wall Street's high rollers who took a dive after embezzling millions and millions and millions." She fiddled with her glass, turning it counterclockwise with its stem on the table. "Ken was an ordinary man, with an ordinary wife, and with two very ordinary children. He simply was not in the ranks of the major players. That he was at the Four Seasons at all was because a rich uncle from the Midwest wanted a glimpse of big-city wining and dining. Ken was all pot roast, mashed potatoes, gravy, beer, and a night in front of the television while he probably wore soiled underpants." She paused for breath. "I did tell you how bitter I feel about all of this!"

She looked up from her glass and nailed me with an accusatory squint as if considering how her vituperation, regarding Ken Salmoth, was sounding to me. "I know you must be thinking all this has to be as lie," she continued. "I assure, it isn't. I admit readily that I just don't understand Gerald's sexual preference for obese men, but now that Stan Greenlyne is in the picture..." She waved a hand in the air as if the connection should be obvious. It wasn't, not entirely; but I was beginning to get a glimpse. I kept very, very quiet. "Gerald was a charmer, as you know, and he knew how to use that charm to his sexual advantage. Ask Giuseppe. Ask Stan Greenlyne!"

"Stan Greenlyne!?" all I dared risk by way of encouragement.

"You mustn't think Gerald was in seventh heaven simply because Don deZinn offered him something to do to keep him from going to seed behind a desk. He'd had his eye on Stan Greenlyne for a long time. Except Stan wasn't as easily seduced, or as gullible, as Ken Salmoth. The latter having only needed a hint that Gerald had quite a few spare dollars to invest. Stan required a more sophisticated approach. Winning Stan over required a longer wait and a lot of good luck. Not that I would be surprised if Gerald hadn't actually planted the idea with Don to use Gerald as middleman between Don and Greenlyne, leading Don to think the idea his own."

For the load this lady was getting off her chest, she should have been down to a twenty-eight-A bra. And she wasn't finished, either. Though, now, she shifted to conjecture.

"What if Gerald came on really strong, and Stan became very upset? Or, what if Stan succumbed to temptation and regretted it? Are either of those as much a motive for murder as Ken Salmoth found his seduction a motive for suicide?"

I didn't buy it. "Did you ever run across a copy of BALLING BUDDIES, or RIDING MY BROTHER'S HORSE?" I asked. I was certain she hadn't. "Stan wasn't always at the top of the heap, you know. He started his illustrious career by writing some pretty salacious stuff. Some of it boy-boy, like the two I mentioned. Some people thought it too insider to be anything but roman a clef. I just don't picture Stan being made indignant by a come-on, or repulsed by anything that may or may not have come after. He, no more than Don, denied a checkered history. To the contrary, both capitalized on the fact at every opportunity."

Greta bit her lower lip. "I guess, I must have known that." She sat back, hands flat on the table, and she began to talk business. "I guess I should be glad Stan's not behind all of this. Telaman Press stock wouldn't exactly respond favorably to his being indicted for murder. It did make quite a dip after the shooting. Do you own any shares in Telaman?" I shook my head. "Who handles your portfolio?" she asked.

"Bill Kavan."

She repeated his name. "I don't believe I know him."

"Keeps a low profile."

"I'm wondering if you would be good enough to recommend me. I honestly need someone, now that Gerald's gone. Gerald handled all of that kind of thing for me, even after we separated."

Divorce didn't get more amicable than that.

She scooted forward, leaned over the table, and

lowered her voice. "Do you really believe all of Stan's bullshit about Clem Rollins?"

I was surprised at the "bullshit", but not by the fact that she had come to pretty much the same conclusion as I had.

"Enough not to admit it in public, or in private," I replied.

She nodded agreement, pulled back, and caught the eye of the very alert waiter. "I'm starved. How about you?"

After we ordered, she told me how glad she was we were having a talk. I wasn't sure how glad I was.

"I've kept a lot cooped up," she continued, "and it needed airing before spontaneous combustion." I wondered whether the police wouldn't have been far more appreciative of her insights than I. She followed my line of thought faster than it played across my brain. "I could never have opened up this way to O'Reilly. He'd think Gerald was some kind of pervert, and I couldn't abide that."

I didn't bother to disabuse her. The fact that her husband had gone to bed with Ken Salmoth, Giuseppe d'Este, and Stan Greenlyne wouldn't have phased O'Reilly in the least, or I thought not. Just another manifestation of the pathology of the human condition.

I was tipsy by the end of the meal and was flirting with Greta as outrageously as I had with women in my bad old days. I never have been able to hold my liquor.

"Want me to see you home?" I suggested, feeling a wine-induced boner rising in my crotch.

"I don't think you really want to," she answered. "It's been nearly perfect. Why risk spoiling it?"

She was right, of course. I put her in a cab and myself in another. Once home, I had another drink I didn't need and would later blame for yet one more evidence of the perversity of la comedie humaine.

I took the cassette from my safe. I put it into the machine and pushed Play. A chair was there to catch me when I fell backward.

Chapter Ten

My secretary's name is Stella, and she hates it (almost as much as I hate Stud). "I get a lot of ribbing about an airhead secretary in some forties movie," she said, "and I'm sick of it." We call her "Stell", and Betty adores her. A great pest she often is, but a screen against the importune. She buzzed me.

"Mr. Greenlyne is here and insists on seeing you. I've told him I can schedule him for four o'clock, but..."

Well, well! "I believe I can spare a few moments now to accommodate Mr. Greenlyne, Stell. Why don't you send him..."

Stan collided with the swinging half-door between the waiting room and the outer officer where Stell reigned supreme, thumped across the carpet, and barreled into my office like a rhino in heat. His charging advance was halted by my desk. His face came within inches of mine.

"What the hell have you done!?" he roared. More

peppermint breath.

"Done?" Stan needed a good whiff of my innocent incredulity. I was going to have to navigate some stormy passages, and I decided to do that the way I knew best. "Done?" I repeated, this time with emphasis.

"Put me in the electric chair and pulled the switch!"

"Oh?" More innocence.

"Stood me on the scaffold, put the noose around my neck, and tripped the trapdoor! You told Rollins I never left the tape with you."

As if I hadn't guessed what he was doing here, huffing and puffing and bumbling about. "Which is exactly what I told you I'd do. Can I help it if you didn't believe me?"

"Clem Rollins had me picked up outside The Green Grocer on the Park." Stan was referring to a posh new restaurant off Central Park West, and from the black clouds roiling about his head, I gathered he had been "picked up" before he'd had his lunch. He pulled back and folded his arms across his chest. "So much for police protection!" he said in hissed disgust. "Cops caught with their heads up their collective asshole."

"Talk to O'Reilly. Complain. Maybe he can assign a couple more men to you."

"Why are you doing this?" Stan asked pleadingly. He saw that roaring and thrashing about were going to get him nowhere.

"Why? Because I gave you a helping hand, and you took advantage. You like to call the shots? Then call them. But I don't have to deal with the results."

Stan continued standing. A wrecking ball might not have budged him, but I was betting money I could. "Sit down, Greenlyne."

Two chairs and the couch escaped devastation. A third chair just barely managed to support Stan's bulk without collapsing into a heap of splinters. I rang Betty on the intercom.

"Would you bring in the package for Mr. Greenlyne, please."

"Draqual, I..."

I silenced him with a finger against my lips. Betty was there in seconds. She carried a silver-coated box with the famous Draqual logo on its lid. I flipped the box open and spread the tissue. "Canary yellow, Stan. Just as you requested."

"What in hell are you talking about?"

"Did you, or did you not, place a phone order for a slip, canary yellow? Remember, I told you a proper fit might require extensive – and expensive – panel inserts?"

"You're joking, right?"

"And the price is really quite reasonable,

considering."

"I'm not here to buy a fuckin' woman's silk slip."

"Just leave us, please, Betty." Mock seriousness. "I'm sure Mr. Greenlyne and I will be able to work out this little, uh, contretemps. And I apologize for our guest's rather crude expletive." Betty wasn't the only one who could be pompous.

On her way out the door, she hung the slip on a rack. She was making a valiant effort to keep a straight face.

"Fifty thousand," I informed Stan.

"Fifty thousand what?"

"Dollars. For the slip."

"You're fuckin' crazy!"

"Fifty thousand. Take it or leave it. But if you leave it, I'll be more than a little disappointed. It's a special order, after all. Normally, we might move it on to alternative customers. But you'll admit that our options for this particular item are extremely limited. Except, perhaps, for the Hamiltons who might possibly be able to use it as their daughter's wedding pavilion. It would go marvelously with Hillary's color scheme."

"This is blackmail!"

"I would prefer to call it first-round negotiations."

"There's a second round?"

"You provide another fifty thousand, and I provide

you with a certain piece of merchandise which turned up one evening, uninvited and unwanted, at my apartment."

"You've not destroyed it, then?" an audible sigh.

"You could always make another, right?" I answered. But he let that one fly over his head. "However, I would advise you to save yourself the effort."

"A hundred grand?" he asked. He was calming down a bit and beginning to sound as if this wasn't such a bad bargain after all.

"Not only for a Draqualian-silk slip and a cassette, remember. But, also, as compensation to me for all the bullshit; payback for your egotistical presumption that I'd willingly let myself be sucked into whatever the game it is you think you're playing with Clem Rollins. And you'd better believe it's a pretty dangerous one."

"You listened to the tape!" Sam exclaimed. Surprise. "You did, didn't you?"

"So much for your estimation of my iron-like willpower. Having had a little too much to drink had something to do with it, of course."

My cards were on the table, and they looked like a Royal Flush to me. "For a mere hundred grand, you are free to resume arrangements to hand over the cassette to Clem," I continued. "The only difference is that I'll no longer be a player in your little charade. Except, of course, by my silence." I decided to drop the clangor. "Which doesn't guarantee that Clem won't find out from somebody else that you're peddling phony merchandise."

"What do you mean, phony!?"

"A pretty good fake," I admitted. "One that might fool even Clem Rollins. But you took a big risk in thinking I'd resist the temptation that killed the proverbial cat."

"I don't know what in hell you're talking about!"

"Stan, that's about the third time you've said that, and you're beginning to sound like a mynah. You know damn well what I'm talking about, but I'll accept your premise. It's going to cost you, though."

"You're telling me the tape isn't real?" he asked. He wanted his money's worth.

"The tape is a tape. It's what's on it that's in question."

"How so, in question?"

"You really need me to spell it out?"

"How is the tape in goddamn question?" Glass panes rattled.

"It's not Don. You almost got it right, but not quite. The intonation and reflection are just a tad off. No clever asides, where Don would have put them. Good enough, I suppose, to fool someone who had never heard Don tell his tales of high adventure in the fleshpots, and at length. But not good enough to fool me. As for Gerald, as interviewer, it might be his voice, or maybe not. I didn't know Gerald all that well, now did I?"

"I swear to God, the tape is one turned over to me by Don and Gerald. Why the fuck would I fake a tape with all that shit on it about Rollins? Do I look suicidal?" How he looked was fat and sweaty.

"Fake or real. Turned over to you by Don, by Gerald, or doctored by you after the fact. However the way, I'm out of it." Dr. Melissa would have been proud. "And you're going to pay me for my exit."

"As if I carry around a hundred grand in pocket change."

"A personal check will do."

"You're kidding!"

"You are good for it, aren't you?"

He produced a checkbook from the inside pocket of his suit jacket. His Mont Blanc fountain pen came next. He didn't need my desk; he used his lap. He flipped the check across the desk with surprising precision.

"Well?" He was suddenly impatient.

I rang for Betty. She was there in a flash. Perhaps Stan expected her to hand him the tape. Sorry, Stan! Now emblazoned in letters of gold thread beneath the rampant dragons of the Draqual Coat of Arms: Duped No More!

"Run this next door, please, will you, Betty, and have our friend see that these funds are transferred immediately. Then give me a call from the bank so I can make Mr. Greenlyne the official owner of a genuine Draqual original that's bound to turn quite a few heads at the next drag ball."

Betty glided out quietly, and Stan and I sat in silence. Stan grimaced, but his mind was elsewhere. I couldn't figure out definitely what the bastard was up to; but I did know that, whatever it was, by virtue of Stan's mischievous temperament, it was going to be devious and dangerous.

When Stan left, a hundred grand poorer, he took the silk slip and the tape with him. (I'd removed the cassette from my desk drawer and held it up ostentatiously before slipping it between the tissue in the Draqual-logo box). He didn't say good-bye.

After Stan had stormed out, I busied myself with choosing a piece of lady's lingerie from among those in the storeroom where we kept odds and ends from previous shows. Pieces which, for one reason or another, hadn't been sold. Hadn't looked just exactly right on the customers who could afford them. Looked stunning on someone who couldn't afford them. Too avant-garde to please. Not avant-garde enough. Pieces that, with additional work, might yet walk off the selling-room floor. Pieces that were simply not up to standard and never would be. Not even Draqual Fashions sold one-hundred percent of its collection one-hundred percent of the time.

I chose a pale pink negligee with a dark pink appliqué bodice. I didn't know why it had never sold; it was one of my favorites: first-class workmanship and beautiful. For the purpose I had in mind, its retail price was a bit steeper than anything I'd originally intended, but I'd just pocketed a hundred grand and could be generous. I folded it, wrapped it in protective tissue, put it in a Draqual-logo box, tied it off with color-coordinated silk ribbon, and cabbed my way uptown to St. Luke's Hospital.

Paul was out of bed and walking around now, and he looked better – but not much. I needn't have been concerned that he wouldn't remember me. When he unwrapped the package and saw what was inside, his bruised eyes opened as wide as they were able.

"It's fucking gorgeous!" he said.

The contrast would be amazing and somewhat (often very) startling to anyone not used to the scene: a grown man, with stubby black beard, hairy legs, hairy arms, and hairy chest, holding a filmy piece of silk against his muscular body to check for proper size. (Paul/Paula's measurements were on file at my office).

"Glad you like it, Paul. But it won't make your cuts and bruises heal any faster."

Continuing to hold the negligee to his body, he looked me straight in the eye. "It's a bribe, isn't it?" he said. He didn't hand the negligee back, though. Not yet, anyway.

"It's a gift. No strings. A deep apology for having inadvertently sent a sadistic policeman to your door."

"I really don't know where Jack and Glennis are. I would have told the cop after even just the first hint that he would knock me around if I didn't cooperate!"

"It's a gift," I emphasized.

"And if I should hear something, somewhere down the line?"

"Then, this could be considered a bribe; it depends on how you choose to act on whatever you may hear." We left it at that.

Back at the office, I returned a call from my broker. "Bill? Stud."

"I've had a meet with Greta Kaney. Looks good. Looks damned good." Bill was what one called a woman's man.

"So, you're very welcome to the referral!"

"Although it'll be hard to match her husband's track record."

"On the money, was he?" I asked.

"Surprisingly often," Bill replied. "Then, anchormen are well-placed to hear things, wouldn't you agree?"

"There're indications Gerald played investments from a stacked deck?" Bill and I were no strangers to the occasional profits to be made from insider information.

"Enough so that you might consider purchase of a few pieces of Telaman Press stock," Bill replied. I waited. Bill went on. "Just before he was killed, Gerald Kaney made some fairly large purchases of Telaman for his wife and for his own portfolio. Since then, there's been no obvious activity on the board to indicate a possible large upswing for the immediate future. The recent flurry and dip is quite logically attributed to Stan Greenlyne's having been shot at. Before Gerald's death, there was just enough additional trading to point to something, but I don't have a clue as to what. Might have been a potential something that simply fizzled. Nobody seems to know anything more concrete – or at least they say they don't. Publishing never was my bailiwick."

"Could have been possible insider anticipation of the release of Don deZinn's book," I ventured.

"You know Greenlyne, don't you?" Bill asked. Turnabout was fair play.

"That's what the papers say," I replied.

"Has he dropped any clues as to whether the book is salvageable?"

"No. And not because I've failed to ask him."

"What do you think?"

What I thought was that Stan was definitely up to something. What I said was: "I think you should buy as much Telaman stock as I have immediate cash reserves to cover. That'll include an additional hundred thousand dollars that I'll have transferred to my brokerage account within the hour."

I could unload later if there was no upward momentum. But, of course, if Stan's lights were suddenly snuffed by a better-aimed barrage of gunfire, Telaman stock would nose-dive even farther. I would just have to depend on Stan's excellent record of survival to keep that from happening.

Chapter Eleven

I slid the designs and silk samples into the top drawer of my desk, folded my hands atop the desk, took a deep breath, and waited the last few seconds of the two minutes I'd asked Stell to give me before showing O'Reilly into my office. Stell buzzed me two times – our signal. O'Reilly came in. He looked every bit as close to burnout as Greta Kaney had surmised. The bags under his eyes were puffier than I remembered. There was a tick of black beard on his left jawline that he'd missed when shaving. His hair was mussed.

"You said this was important," I said in greeting.

"Have you ever seen this?" He produced a cassette from one pocket of his rumpled suit jacket.

"Lots of them."

"I mean this one in particular."

"Not that I can tell from here. Is 'Seen by Stud Draqual' scrawled somewhere on the cover?"

"Can I use your tape deck?" There was no hiding the entertainment center I'd had installed along one wall of my office.

"I have better things to do that listen to Muzak, Inspector. Like run a business."

"This won't take long."

O'Reilly adjusted the volume, and the voices came through:

First Voice: "So what was it exactly that Clem Rollins liked to do?"

Second Voice: "Have me dress up."

F.V.: "You mean, dressing up like going to church or out to dinner?"

S.V.: "No, full drag. Wig. Makeup. Nylons. Spiked heels. Garter belt. Panties. Slip. Evening dress. Clem liked blue." (I knew Clem liked red, but I kept that to myself).

F.V.: "And?"

S.V.: "And, then, he'd get down on all fours, naked as a jay, and have me fuck him without my removing a stitch. Just shift the crotch of my panties to one side."

"Recognize either voice?" asked O'Reilly.

I raised my hand, asking for more time. There was no

way I wanted him to know I'd heard this before. The question niggling the back of my mind was how O'Reilly had gotten hold of the tape – and from whom. The last I'd seen, it was in the box along with Stan's canary-colored silk tent.

F.V: "Clem got off on that, did he?"
S.V.: "What really got him off was playing barnyard."
F.V.: "Barnyard?"

"Maybe Gerald Kaney," I responded.

S.V.: "...a couple of my friends. Clem had these papier-mâché masks – three bulls, one cow. He'd be the cow; we'd be the bulls and fuck him, one after the other. Clem mooed like poor Old Bossy."

"Someone pretending to be Don deZinn," I told O'Reilly.
O'Reilly switched off the machine. "Pretending to be?"
"It's not Don," I repeated. "Whoever it is almost got it right, but not quite."
"As it turns out, the interviewer is not Gerald Kaney,

either." He popped the cassette out of the machine and re-pocketed it. "Any guesses?"

"Don't you have electronics people who work on this sort of thing? Voiceprints and all that? Match-ups from tapes handed over to Greenlyne by Don and Gerald?"

"This is supposed to be one of those tapes handed over to Greenlyne by Don and Gerald."

"Supposed?" We continued to agree.

"As far as we can determine, the rest are genuine, but not this one. For comparison, we had Gerald on network newscasts and Don from a TV interview."

"From what I just heard, Clem Rollins might be the man to help you track down these clowns."

"The clown," O'Reilly said, emphasizing the singular. "Name's Richy Biglow."

"The missing comedian?"

"That information courtesy of that anonymous source I was busy with when Paul Cortland was questioned." O'Reilly sounded as if he was still rankling over my reaction to Paul Cortland's treatment at the hands of one of O'Reilly's cops. If so, that was good enough for me for the moment.

"I sure as hell wouldn't want to be Richy Biglow when Clem Rollins gets wind of this," I said.

"You wouldn't want to be Richy Biglow, period. He's

dead."

"I thought he was just missing."

"I thought so, too, until a couple of hours ago. He turned up, bullet hole in the temple. Ritual killing, it looks like. Ballistics say it's the same weapon that killed deZinn and Kaney – and put the hole in Stan Greenlyne's expensive car upholstery."

"You're kidding!"

"The department is as leaky as a sieve, and I expect all of this has reached the media by now. If, through some miracle it hasn't, I'd appreciate you keeping it to yourself. I'm telling you only because of your connection with everybody involved – except Richy Biglow." Pause. "You didn't know Biglow, did you?"

"No."

"Your connection with the others makes me hopeful you still may be able to shed some light on the situation."

"Inspector O'Reilly, I design, make, and sell women's underwear. What you need is input from Sam Spade, Perry Mason, Jessica Fletcher. I don't know squat."

"Stan Greenlyne says you've heard this cassette before." So, that's where he got it!

"Stan Greenlyne is mistaken." Up yours, Stan!

"Anything on that tape sound like anything Don ever told you?" Trick question. I was learning. He may be near burnout, but he was still one very clever bastard.

"Hard to tell, since I assume what I just heard isn't everything on the tape. What you played rings no bells, though. And I strongly suspect I would have remembered any of that."

O'Reilly thought a moment. "This next is all inside stuff," he finally said, "and I'm telling you because I think you can be trusted to keep it to yourself. Also, I think you'll still be able to help us out in spite of how you feel about the Paul Cortland thing. So... my boss figures Greenlyne was used by Galin Tarbothi to set Rollins up for a fall. Greenlyne's convincing when he says he's never heard of Tarbothi, but then he wouldn't have had to."

"I've never heard of Tarbothi."

"There's been some friction between Rollins and him – old blood versus new, old ways versus new. Old story. New players."

"Rollins is supposed to go under because of a doctored tape? Give me a break!"

"Sandwiched in with the originals, who'd know? Maybe you, because of your close relationship with Don. But you weren't supposed to hear it. And you think Stan would be able to tell the difference between this and the real thing? You think I would, even though I've verified it as phony? Biglow's career wasn't in the shit because he wasn't a good mimic, but because he was too good. Ask Johnny Carson, or is Johnny still alive?"

"So, the lies slip through, get transcribed, then published," I summarized what I thought was his scenario. Then, I embellish with some thoughts of my own: "Rollins sues. Experts are brought in. The truth comes out. Rollins is vindicated. Telaman Press is out big bucks for libel, not to mention the loss of its reputation."

"You see Rollins sitting around for a lengthy trial? Lasting months? Years? All that time the garbage you've just heard stays there, in print, for anyone and everyone to see and read? What kind of image is that for a Mafia don? On his hands and knees, screwed silly by drag queens and mooing like a cow? Rollins isn't young. He wants a slow and easy fade-out into retirement. He's going to deal with all the shit this tape is going to cause, without having a stroke or heart attack? Not likely!"

"How'd Tarbothi squeeze the fake tape in with the real ones?" I wanted to know.

"Please, Mr. Draqual. It's your turn to get serious!"

Yes, even I could see that if Stan Greenlyne could circumvent my apartment's security system, Tarbothi could sure as hell crack whatever Gerald's place had had to offer.

"What I think," I replied, "is that maybe Don and Gerald were killed to keep the truth from coming out during reads of early book proofs."

"I don't have any trouble with that," O'Reilly responded.

"Or, maybe Don and Gerald were killed before enough tapes were made to make a book," I continued.

O'Reilly didn't confirm or deny; so, I tried this: "Does Greenlyne have the book in the pipeline?" Clever boy-detective still at work. Clever seeker-of-fortune still greedy.

O'Reilly wasn't buying. "I'd say that was Telaman Press business."

Undaunted, I soldiered on. "So, now you arrest Tarbothi?"

"Don't I wish. Pieces fit, but he's too smart."

"I'd like to help, but..." As far as I was concerned, this Tarbothi business had put me out of the equation; but, O'Reilly rambled on.

"I have reports of Paul Cortland cutting a rather dashing figure, these days, among the patients at St. Luke's."

"It was the least I could do."

"Pretty expensive gift, or so a lady friend of mine,

who seems to know, tells me."

Paul doesn't have a clue where Jack Fornal and Glennis Rhynne are."

"Which doesn't mean that tomorrow the information won't drop into his suddenly silk-covered lap."

"Which doesn't mean he'll come running to me, either."

"More likely to you than to me."

I couldn't deny that. "Whose fault is that?"

"Certain people won't come forward, even when they're treated with kid gloves."

Brutality didn't make any exceptions to that rule any more likely. Someone who had his act together would surely have known one of his men had a castrated nephew, and that someone wouldn't have let that cop near Paul Cortland. I understood that. I felt O'Reilly did, too, and that made me go easier.

"What about a Fornal-Rollins or Fornal-Tarbothi connection?" I asked.

"Jack paid a percentage to Rollins for the privilege of peddling Glennis' ass on the street, but that money went through channels. Never mano a mano, never directly from Jack to the man on top. No more than most of you, in the rag trade, deal directly with a capo. You're a possible exception, of course." I knew what was coming, and it did: "Want to talk about your recent visit to Long Island?"

"You have me followed? If you did, I want you to know right now I'll..."

"Just calm down, Mr. Draqual. We observe Rollins, on and off. Long-standing habits are hard to break. You just happened by."

"His wife's a Draqual customer. She invited me for morning coffee. Her business is worth a trip to Long Island. Rollins happened to be there. He does live there after all."

"If you say so."

"I do. Tell me about Jack Fornal's rap sheet. I presume he has one." If O'Reilly had told me one inside story, maybe he'd tell me another.

"I'd rather hear about Rollins and you."

"Think ALICE IN WONDERLAND, substituting coffee for tea."

"Mr. Draqual, I'm working very hard on this case, and I don't have much room for your continuing hostility and sarcasm. So, let's get on with it, okay? All right... Jack was an incorrigible prepubescent. Juvie records, including his, are sealed. He's an equally bad-ass adult. Ordered into the Army by a California judge. Ordered out by Uncle Sam; something about the death of a prostitute in Munich, Jack having moonlighted as her pimp. Been here in the City about a year. Purely minor league. Couple of assault and batteries, petty theft. None stuck, so no jail time. Nothing with a gun, but Army service records suggest he would know how to use one. Now... anything you can do to help us, I'd very much appreciate."

* * *

As soon as O'Reilly left, I called Broker Bill and placed another order to buy Telaman Press stock. A non-answer from O'Reilly, about the possibility of a deZinn book, did not deter me.

Could Stan have engineered any or all of these little dances to jack up eventual book sales? I immediately discounted this as pretty absurd. Hardly enough money, surely, in a single book, no matter what the possibilities, to warrant multiple-murder. I continued to ruminate until Betty came into the office with the same gloomy countenance with which she'd announced that Paul Cortland was in the hospital, bruised and bleeding.

"I'm here to listen, Betty. Might was well spit it out. Bad news is seldom any better by pretending it isn't." My avuncular Uncle Stud voice.

"It's Kyle Kaiser."

"Our fitter is in the ER, calling my name?" I ventured. "Reporters talking police brutality?"

"He hasn't shown for work in days. He hasn't called in. I can't get him on his phone. He's had a good attendance record so far," Betty insisted. "This is out of character."

"Anyone listed in his personnel file to notify in case of possible emergency?"

"Someone called Jerry Quay. Woman who answered that number, though, hasn't a clue. Tenant before her, she thinks, was named Sarah Porceley."

At least this was an administrative problem for which I could provide an adequate solution and meet with pithy decisions. "Miss Petersen: a sub-fitter. See if she's available for permanent status. If Kyle turns up with a reasonable explanation for his absence – kidnapped by aliens and didn't have access to a phone, for example – we'll take that into consideration and act from there."

If I thought that a masterful resolution, Betty didn't. I could tell. By looking.

"Kyle's a dear friend of yours?" I put out feelers.

Betty shook her head.

"An old boyfriend? A recent lover? An old boyfriend of a recent lover? A brother of an old boyfriend? Mugged by a transvestite trucker in the men's room at Grand Central? You will stop me when I'm anywhere close?"

"I saw Kyle kissing Don deZinn in Cubicle J a few days before Don was murdered."

"Jesus, Betty!" Talk about revelations! I calmed down a bit when I took in Betty's rather hang-dog look. "Okay, okay, I understand. Do you think O'Reilly knows?"

"If he does, he's dug it out all by himself. I certainly didn't tell him. I figured it was none of his business, although I know it is, of course."

"Don is dead, Betty," I reminded her. "Not of natural causes, I need hardly add."

"When Paul Cortland got pounded, I was more convinced than ever that I should keep Kyle and Don's secret locked away in my own little pea-brain."

"Except that Kyle is now missing, yes?"

"He could be sick."

"And not answering his phone?"

"Too sick to answer."

"Way too ill to survive homophobic cops pounding at his door, slapping him around, hauling his ass to jail, or to St. Luke's?"

"I thought I'd drop by his place tonight, on my way home."

"Not necessarily a good idea, Betty."

"It would be harmless. Fellow worker. Concerned. Checking up."

"Fag-hag. Concerned. Checking up. Maybe." I checked my watch. "But I can't risk anything happening to you. Not only do I love you, but you're also the only one around here who knows anything these days. I, on the other hand..."

"Maybe we should call O'Reilly, after all," Betty said.

And maybe I should call Dr. Melissa!

"I'll stop by Kyle's place, and I'll just do a little glance-over," I said. "If I get any funny feelings, I'll call O'Reilly immediately." Call Dr. Melissa? "If Kyle's in bed with a cold, no sense making him feel worse by siccing O'Reilly's goons on him."

Dr. Melissa, smiling: "You can't fool me, buster. It's the famously classic I-am-a-camera syndrome."

* * *

Kyle lived on the third floor of a four-floor walk-up. His name was on the tenant listing, and I buzzed. There was no answer. I had not read Telaman Press' UNSAFE BEHIND LOCKED DOORS, by Cleveland Moore, so I buzzed the super who wore carpet slippers; baggy jeans, held up with suspenders; sweater, much too large, with holes in the elbows. Pipe. Eager to help.

Mr. Gorff, though, hadn't seen Mr. Kaiser in weeks, months, long before Kyle had dropped out of work. "Only coming-and-going. You know how it is? Didn't pay him much mind. Non-bothersome young man." A genuine compliment, by the sound of it. "Can't say that for most. You wouldn't believe the problems in this old building." Problems years in the making, tenants expecting immediate attention. Burst pipes, cold radiators, smelly johns, clogged drains, roaches...

I suggested that Kyle might be bedridden and unable to get to the phone. "Shouldn't we check to make sure everything is okay?"

Gorff had a passkey.

The bed was empty and tidy. Dishes washed, dried, and out of sight. Phone on its hook and working. No unopened mail. No newspapers piled in front of the door. Food in the frig: cottage cheese, gone moldy; carton of milk, not yet sour... Open and splayed, spine-up-on-the-coffee-table: a copy of Telaman Press' STORM FEEDINGS. Best-selling story of a South Carolina zoo keeper who'd kept his carnivorous charges alive, during and after Hurricane Hugo, by feeding them human meat.

"Gorff, you in there!?" Not Kyle.

"Yeah. What's the trouble, Slykes!?"

"My toilet, what else? It overflows, even as we speak."

"If I find another of your wife's sanitary napkins..."

"The bitch left me two weeks ago, and nothing's down there but my piss and bran-softened shit."

Gorff turned to me. "Set as many locks as you can when you leave, will you? I'll take care of the others on my way back down."

Slykes and Gorff trudged heavily up the stairs. Water pipes gurgled as, somewhere, a toilet continued to overflow in greeting.

I could be a burglar. All of Kyle's possessions could be hauled away by my accomplices, waiting in a van, and/or ripped off by me. Except, I wasn't a burglar. I was just a man, with no accomplices, who had a sudden urge to piss.

Dr. Melissa: "You saw that closed bathroom door and thought – what? 'I need to take a leak.' Better still: 'I wonder if the body's in the bathtub?'"

I sniffed the air. No decomposing corpses, not that I'd ever smelled even one. Redolence of after-shave: Eau de Homme. I put my ear to the bathroom door. What I expected to hear, I had no idea. I turned the knob. Slowly. Pushed gently. Squinted so that whatever scene

I encountered wouldn't be too jarring and horrible to contemplate.

The bathroom was empty. The curtain around the tub was pulled back to reveal nothing more than a ring of scum deposited by a drained bath. There was a swoosh of air behind me, and a swift movement glimpsed out of the corner of my eye, as I started to turn. Suddenly, my head hurt – bad! My knees buckled, and I hit the floor.

Chapter Twelve

I didn't know what hit me (a flashlight, as it turned out), only vaguely aware of the swift movement that brought it up behind me. And I didn't know how long I had been out, only that there had been nightmares.

Awareness slowly returned, but not with any immediate realization that I'd been coldcocked.

I heard Kyle Kaiser's voice from a distance: "I managed to catch Mr. Draqual just as he was leaving."

I heard a second voice and tried to place it: "He was really concerned about you. You never called in sick or nothing."

"My mother had a heart attack." Kyle's mother was dead. How did I know that? "I didn't think of anything except getting to her as fast as I could."

"She going to be okay?"

"She's home from the hospital now but weak as a baby. We kids..." Kyle was an only child. Who'd told me that and when? "...are going to take turns watching out for her, so I may not be around for a few days. I'd appreciate it if you would look in on the apartment, every now and then, to make sure it's still here."

"Sure, I'll do that." Gorff. Mr. Gorff. Where did I know Gorff?

Why was it so damned dark? Maybe it was because my eyes were shut!

Why did my head hurt so damned much? Maybe it was because I'd received a whack that would have done Lizzy Borden proud.

Who or what made that sudden, low growl? I did!

Why did I imagine myself a pig with an apple in my mouth, ready for carving? I was gagged!

"Thank God!" Kyle now above me and closer. "I thought I'd killed you." That made two of us. I still wasn't certain he hadn't.

He lifted me gently into a sitting position. Three very bright white stars exploded across the blackness. The same white comets had streaked across the darkness when I'd come to after my fall onto the rocks of the Colorado River; when I'd regained consciousness after my head had intercepted a small dislodged boulder on a Tibetan alp; when I'd finally come around after a disastrous tumble from my horse during a polo match...

"Promise not to yell, and I'll take out the gag," Kyle said. Blackness became blacker. "Mr. Draqual?" Gentle slaps across my face. "Please! Don't conk out on me again." He removed the rag – the apple from this pig's mouth.

"Jesus, my head!" was what I wanted to say, but it didn't come out sounding even close. My mouth was dry and linty.

"I didn't know it was you," Kyle said. "I thought you were someone sent by..." He didn't finish the sentence.

"By...? Go on!"

"Try to open your eyes."

"You thought I'd been sent by... try to open your eyes." A string of nonsense syllables making nonsense words.

"Come on, Mr. Draqual! Try!" Try what? "I don't want to leave you until I'm sure you're okay." Was there a hospital close by? "I've left the knots loose. You'll have to work at them a little, so try to concentrate." Try to open my eyes? Try to concentrate? "I've moved the phone down here, beside you on the floor, so you can get to it more easily." What phone? What floor? "Come on, Mr. Draqual!" He laid his hands on my shoulders and gave me a gentle shake.

"Damn, my head!" I wanted to massage the ache, but

my wrists were bound. I tried to open my eyes, but someone had glued them together. I tried again. Excruciatingly bright light.

"Mr. Draqual!" Another shake. "I've got to go."

"Go where?"

Kyle finally came into focus, squatting on the floor beside me, registered in blacks and whites, then muted tones, and finally in full color.

"You're supposed to be sick," I told him and finally sounded human.

"I'll be more than sick if I'm not careful – and if I don't get away from here fast."

More brilliant light dawned over Marblehead. "You'll be dead, right?" Gerald Kaney was dead. Don deZinn was dead. "Seen kissing Don in a dressing room," I added.

"Christ!"

I saw him better now: red hair; pale, freckled skin; green eyes; pert upturned nose; full mouth. "Rubbing your crotches together."

"Christ!" he said again. "How many other people know?"

"Know what?" Muddy reasoning, cloudy thinking. Not yet quite crystal clear.

"Damn it, Mr. Draqual, this could be life or death for

me!"

"Why the fuck hit me on the head?" It seemed we'd had this discussion before, but I wasn't sure. "Here I sit on your floor, clonked, gagged and tied. And you're worried about your pretty skin?"

"I thought you were someone else... or someone sent by someone else."

"By whom?" Yes, we'd talked about this before. I couldn't remember Kyle's answer, so my question was still valid.

"If you don't know, then I wouldn't be doing you any real big favor by telling you."

"What exactly do you know about Don's murder?"

"Maybe nothing." That was certainly noncommittal. "Maybe a lot." That had possibilities. "But I'm not taking any chances. I've got to fade into the woodwork fast. Your bad luck and mine, too, for you to be here, just when I'd come back to get a few things. Now, I'm going to put the gag back in your mouth."

"Come on, Kyle. What if I vomit? That bang on my head has made me feel pretty sick. I could drown in my own puke. You'd be to blame. They'd have you up for murder. Put you away. Strap you in the chair. Pull the..."

"Sorry." He stuffed the sock into my mouth, not ramming it, rather easing it in a little at a time. Thanks a lot, asshole! Don't come back to me begging for your job back!

"I won't make it tight. It shouldn't take long to spit it out. I'm really sorry."

He ran hurriedly out the door, and I heard him on the stairs.

"I have to take a leak, you bastard!" I screamed after him.

Despite Kyle's assurances, and a lot of my wiggling, it still took a long, long time to free my wrists of rope and my mouth of spit-saturated sock. Just as I did manage, the phone rang and literally scared the piss (albeit only a short squirt), out of me.

"Yes?" My mouth still didn't work right.

"Kyle Kaiser?"

"Stud Draqual."

"For God's sake!" Betty hadn't recognized my voice, and no wonder. "Is Kyle all right?"

"Kyle's fine," I said. Or, maybe, not so fine, depending on how one looked at it. But there was no point in shaking Betty up with tales of rope, sock, and flashlight-to-the-head.

"Paul Cortland called. Said it's important that he reach you. Something about payback time."

"How long ago was that?"

"Actually, he just hung up."

"You have the hospital phone number?"

"He's not at the hospital. Discharged yesterday."

"Did he leave a number?"

"Home phone. Got a pen and paper?"

I fumbled around for both in my jacket pocket. "Yes. Shoot!" Not a good choice of word, considering.

In my opinion, Betty couldn't relay the numbers fast enough, because: "Look, Betty, I've really got to see a man about a race horse." I broke the connection and, unsteady on my feet, barely made it to the bathroom in time.

* * *

Paul picked up on the second ring. "I've heard from Glennis," he said.

I shut my eyes to concentrate but I decided they were better left open. I was still feeling pretty woozy, holding down nausea.

Luckily, I didn't have to prod him. "Jack beat the shit out of her," Paul continued. "He's done it before. She's managed to get to a friend's place."

"This friend have a name?"

"Glennis wouldn't say. She's really pissed, though.

Always is, after."

Pissed enough to have told you where Jack is?"

Paul gave me the name of a hotel, not far away, and a room number. "Whatever you plan to do, I'd do it fast," Paul continued. "Glennis usually doesn't stay pissed for long. I've seen her back in that bastard's arms before her blood clots."

After I hung up, I called O'Reilly. The switchboard patched me through. He wanted to know where I was. He told me to stay put; he'd get back to me.

I stood, reeled more than was comfortable, placed a hand against the wall for a few seconds, to still the vortex, and headed for the front door.

Dr. Melissa: "Still in the frying pan but ready for the fire, huh!?"

Me (to me): "If I get teetery on the stairs, I'll go back to Kyle's apartment. If I can't hail a cab within two minutes, I'll go back. If my mind blanks out the name of the hotel, I'll go back."

I was fine on the stairs. I got a taxi right away. The name of the hotel flowed smoothly off my tongue. I reached my destination in no time at all – a block short of Jack's hotel. Clearer thinking, now, with logical self-protective reasoning.

I crossed the street so as to approach the hotel from

the opposite side. I had no intention of getting too close, but I wanted to be close enough not to miss whatever action might come down. If anybody wanted to talk about payback – well, I deserved a ringside seat for O'Reilly's little show.

I chose a convenient doorway. The storefront was boarded up and covered with graffiti. Typical of this neighborhood, but no worse than any other, once out of mid-town East Side.

I waited. And I waited. And I wondered what the fuck was going on. And I waited some more. But enough was enough!

Just because I moved from the protection of the doorway, though, didn't mean I intended to go into the hotel, march up the stairs, and do O'Reilly's job for him. I only wanted to get closer to see if I was missing anything.

Grandmother: "Curiosity killed the you-know-what!"

Me: "Yeah, but satisfaction brought you-know-what..."

The hand came from behind me – a big hand. Splayed fingers covered my mouth and nose and most of my face. I was yanked backwards, to one side, and into the deep shadows of a once entirely brick-veneered alcove.

Chapter Thirteen

He had me securely locked against him. There was no give to his body. His left arm, like a strong metal vise, was slung around in front of me; it and its accompanying hand pinioned my arms against my sides. His belly ground my butt. His chin wedged over my left shoulder, against my neck; his whisker-stubbled right cheek exerted pressure that kept my head from shaking off his other slab-like hand that anchored over my face.

"Don't fight me, damn it!" A whispered command against my left ear.

I had no choice but to struggle. My brain, deprived of oxygen, sent instructions for survival that didn't include passive resistance. I was suffocating in the airless vacuum between his hand and my face.

I braced my feet and heaved my weight upward and backward. I twisted, bounced, pulled, but to no avail. The man was as solid and rigid as iron.

The shadows into which I'd been forcibly drawn took on the complete blackness of deep caverns where no shapes are ever distinguished, no matter how long one's sight is permitted an attempted adjustment.

"Snap out of it, damn it!" the whisper reached me from a great distance.

I was not conscious of how or when I finally came to be laid flat out on my back. I sat up, coughed, wheezed, and sucked in precious air.

"You bastard!" O'Reilly rasped. He was down on one knee, on the pavement beside me. "Is this what I meant when I told you to stay put?"

"You sonofabitch!" I wheezed. "You nearly killed me!"

"This operation could be shot to hell if Fornal sees you."

"How long has it been since I called you?" I checked my watch but couldn't see it. "An hour? Two?"

"A stakeout like this takes time. What did you expect, for Christ's sake? Spotlights? Sirens? Bullhorns? So Fornal can take hostages and play never-take-him-alive This isn't TV, sport!"

O'Reilly wasn't improving my mood. He wouldn't even be here if it hadn't been for me. It sure as hell wasn't his brilliant police work that had turned the clues. That had been done by a pink silk-and-lace peignoir which I'd given to a battered drag queen.

"Now, stay put, for God's sake – right here! I don't want anybody – get it? anybody! – to know you're within a thousand miles of this place."

As soon as O'Reilly was up and away, I propped myself against a pee-stained wall and shimmied farther across the pavement, so I could see the hotel down and across the broad, busy avenue.

The streetscape looked normal and commonplace... routine for this time of day. I knew there was a police operation in progress, but to my eyes, no one looked like a cop hanging around to nab a suspect. The drunk, propped against a dumpster: a police sergeant? The well-dressed woman, window-shopping: a plainclothes foil? The leather-costumed stud, on the corner: a detective on his umpteenth stakeout? The seemingly teenage kid, bouncing a stained tennis ball off the side of a building: a rookie on his first raid? Hard to tell, and time had come to a complete standstill.

I felt no compulsion to sit around any longer, and I was actually up and moving when O'Reilly exited the hotel. Weaving between two passing cars, he crossed the avenue and came toward me.

"That's what I really like about you, Draqual! Always

William Maltese

willing to cooperate; always ready to help out! Always willing to stay put! You could have queered this whole damn operation, but it doesn't make that much difference at this point... thank God! In case you're interested, there's a little bad news, and a little good news." I waited, albeit none too patiently. "Fornal is dead. Dead too long for me to hassle you for tipping him off by being here in the first place. Shot. Maybe suicide. Maybe not. We have the body. We have a head wound. We have powder burns. We have the gun. What we don't have is the why."

"The poor sucker couldn't live with himself any longer?" I suggested.

"Nothing in his background would suggest an overly sensitive conscience."

"Never-take-me-alive mentality?"

"Dead before we even arrived."

"He could have figured it was only a matter of time before Glennis turned him in."

"Easier to shift base... get out of town. Easier to kill Glennis outright."

"Maybe he thought he'd already killed her. She's in piss-poor condition, according to what I hear."

"Where exactly did Cortland say this poor, beaten gangster's moll is holed up?"

"With a friend."

"I've hopes Paul might be persuaded to elaborate on that."

"And you know just the cop to send to that follow-up interview!"

"Listen, Draqual. We've been through this, over and over. So, please get off my back. Besides, the cop who pounded on Paul Cortland has been suspended and will probably be kicked off the force – that is if I have anything to do with it. Don't you read the papers?"

I was mollified, somewhat, but I still wasn't all that overly willing to forgive and forget. "I'll tell you frankly, O'Reilly, I don't feel much like handing out any more peignoirs to buy your information. Now, if you'll please excuse me, I'm going back to my office to take care of badly-neglected business."

"Amateurs only fuck up the works, anyway," he said – almost to himself.

* * *

Once a safe distance from O'Reilly, I called Dr. Melissa on my cell phone. It wasn't as if she had a full roster these days. She preferred her antiques, modern paintings, Persian rugs, and expensive gewgaws, accumulated during a lifetime of cash inflow from screw-ups like me.

I'd contributed enough to her expensive, and very special tastes, to give me an instantaneous entree to her exclusive salon. She seldom, if ever, turned me down.

"What?" she asked, twenty minutes into our impromptu session. It wasn't that she had misunderstood me in any essentials. She understood only too well. It was, rather, that she seemed to be waiting to hear the punch line of a long, involved, and not very funny joke.

She tapped her pencil on the desk. Twice. Always twice. Never once. Not three, four, or five times. Only twice. Then, she scratched the hairline at her right temple. Never her left. Never the top of her head. Never the back of her neck.

She wore no makeup. The liver spots on the backs of her hands ran amuck. Eyelashes, almost invisible without mascara, blinked against the similar whiteness of her pale, bleached skin. Her lips were so thin as to seem nonexistent without some kind of artificial coloring.

Her polka-dot dress hung loosely on her thin body, its hem frizzled in at least two places.

"I thought you and I had reached the point where it's no longer necessary to play games," she chided. She shook her head, sighed, sat back, and looked much put-upon. Anyone would have thought my tale of high adventure was keeping her from something vastly more important.

I offered a placating sacrifice. "I think what you need is something to perk up your spirits," I said. "How about a Draqual nightie at cost?"

"Fine. I'll be around tomorrow, first thing." An at-cost Draqual teddy had roped her into taking me on in the first place, and her appreciation for fine lingerie remained steadfast. "That takes care of my psyche; now let's get back to yours."

"Look, Dr. Melissa..."

"Doctor DoLittle, if you please!" That routine hadn't changed since the first time I'd seen her. It gave me a sense of reassuring continuity.

"...I had an interesting day. I thought you might be interested as well."

"Oh, I am, indeed." She raised her eyebrows and then lowered them just as rapidly. Her squint hid the chalky porcelain grey of her eyes. "I just wish I didn't have to work so hard for the good parts."

"What good parts?"

She leaned forward, put her elbows on the desk, and pointed her pencil. "How did it feel to have this man tightly against you, in an alleyway?"

"It wasn't an alley. It was a kind of alcove. A piece of wall in a state of collapse, though most of the debris had been hauled away."

"Next, you'll tell me the size of the remaining bricks, their number, their placement in the wall. None of which I particularly want to hear."

"I was suffocating; I couldn't breathe with that asshole O'Reilly's hand over my face."

"His cheek against your cheek. His chest against your back. His belly against your rear end. His arm around your waist."

"Congratulations! You listened."

She let this pass. "What about O'Reilly's cock?"

"Good God, DoLittle! What is it with your permanent case of pecker-on-the-brain?"

"Don't answer a question with a question, Draqual. That's my job!"

"What exactly do you want me to tell you about O'Reilly's cock? I've never seen it, hope never to see it, and can only guess that it was snuggled securely in his BVD's."

"Was it hard?"

"Jesus H. Christ!"

"You felt his chest. You felt his belly. You felt his arm. You felt his hands. You felt his whiskers. Was his cock hard?"

"I don't know; I can't remember."

"I believe you."

I didn't believe her.

"Which doesn't mean," she added, "that you won't remember – someday."

She leaned back and folded her arms across breasts I figured had long ago withered to nothingness. "What you don't understand, Draqual, after all this time, is that it doesn't really mean diddly-squat whether you were aware of O'Reilly's cock or not, or whether or not you knew for a fact that it was hard. I would never presume you gay simply because you tell me that you felt it pressed tightly against you, hard as a rock."

"I tried to stay alive in that alley..."

"Alcove. Of sorts," she corrected. "Provided by the evacuation of two-thousand-six-hundred-and-two red three-by-six tumbled-down bricks."

"Funny!"

"O'Reilly's on a big assignment to nab a killer. He's tense. Is this going to work? Is this going to fail? Are cops going to get hurt? Are innocent bystanders going to suffer? Will he get a promotion? Will he get a reprimand? Suddenly, there you are. Where you shouldn't be. When you shouldn't be. O'Reilly is pissed. You can screw up the entire works. The shooter knows you. Maybe even tried to kill you outside your building.

The killer will wonder what you're doing there. Wonder if you brought the cops along. O'Reilly needs you out of the way. You think his adrenaline isn't flowing? You think adrenaline isn't a powerful aphrodisiac? Have you never gotten a hard-on shooting class-five white-water rapids? Have you never become aroused traversing a hairy stretch of Tibetan mountain? Have you never gotten a stiffy doing whatever it is you rich boys do on those polo ponies?"

She waited for that to sink in. Unlike some shrinks, Dr. Melissa wasn't against doing all the talking; not when she was charging by the hour. Often, I was lucky to get a word in edgewise.

"Ergo," she continued, right along, "O'Reilly with a hard-on – if he had one, that is – doesn't mean, nor did it ever mean, he was hot for your body. You do see that, don't you?"

"Yes," I admitted begrudgingly.

"To hear you tell it, you walk around in a perpetual arousal that doesn't mean you're perpetually hot to trot. In fact, you're to have me believe, quite to the contrary."

"Point taken."

"Speaking of your cock, what condition was it in, during all this?"

"I'm to keep track of the condition of my cock while

I'm being strangled and smothered? You seem to think I was merely being recruited for kinky sex."

"Which doesn't answer my question."

She waited. Waited some more. I'd long since wised up to her game of waiting for the patient – me – to fill in the silences.

"Okay," she finally conceded. "Let's talk about asphyxiation as a sexual stimulant. It's a fact that criminals who, in the good old days, were actually executed for their crimes, often hanged with spontaneous erections. Each year, men hang nooses from doors, stick heads through those nooses, exert the necessary pressure to cut off air to their windpipes, and jack-off while judging, or often misjudging, how close, in their mounting excitement, they are to death's doorstep."

"So, I had an erection. So what?"

"Exactly! So what? It doesn't mean you were excited by the man, even if he was so tightly against you that you felt his hard-on laid out along the crack of your ass."

"Have you ever thought of writing porno, DoLittle? I'm sure Stan Greenlyne might still have an in with a few publishers in that line of business – that is if you should decide to shift careers."

She was good at overlooking my best sarcasm, and also very, very good at swift diversions. "What are your feelings about O'Reilly? And don't bother screaming, because I'm not hard of hearing."

"He's a flatfoot on a case. He could have killed me."

"I've an associate who's very interested in transcendent out-of-body experiences. Do you recall any lights at the end of long, dark tunnels?"

"Maybe we should spend some time talking about your associate." I was being facetious, but she refused to pick up on it.

"Are we close to something you'd just as soon not reveal to anyone, even yourself?" she threw from left field.

"Like what?"

"Tell me what you find unattractive about O'Reilly."

"Why?"

"Humor me."

"He dresses like a small-time college basketball coach. He hates queers."

"How do you know he hates queers?"

"Paul Cortland is queer, and he ended up in the hospital because of O'Reilly, didn't he?"

"For which O'Reilly assumes responsibility only insofar as he unknowingly assigned an officer to the case who had a nephew who... etceteras, etceteras, etceteras."

"He has bags under his eyes big enough to tote

Kentucky. He's too tall. He's going to pot."

"I thought he felt as hard as a brick wall against you."

"So, maybe, he just looks like he's going to pot. And he bites his nails, which I find a particularly disgusting habit."

"How about something you find attractive about him? There must be something."

I provided a good, long pause. I didn't want her to think my response was ready and waiting on the tip of my tongue. "He has a good, rugged jawline."

"Does he have dimples? You like dimples."

"No dimples." What he has is a deep crease.

"How about a cleft chin? You like a cleft chin."

"When did I ever tell you I liked a cleft chin?"

"Do you?"

"His could be deeper. He might try shaving his beard out of it, too."

She pursed her lips. "I've never quite understood... And, maybe, you're far enough along in therapy now to explain how you've managed... and feel free to correct me if I've got this wrong... You were never off with another little boy, showing peepees behind some barn?"

"No." I'd never been near a barn.

"No, or...?"

"Not that I recall."

She rewarded me with a smile so thin-lipped it was hardly evident.

"You never sneaked away to the toolshed with the gardener's son to exchange exploratory feelies?"

Our gardener didn't have a son. "Not that I recall."

"And, locked within the rarefied atmosphere of that New England prep school, alone with all those hot, sweaty boys, with their raging hormones, like you... no upperclassmen who took advantage? Never a worshipful first-former, with innocent but willing little dick or asshole, of whom you took advantage?"

"Not that I recall."

"And while at university..."

"Not that I recall. Not that I recall!" I saved her the effort of any additional hyperbole.

"I guess my real question is: Why not? Most heterosexual men – by the most widely accepted definition of the term – if pressed, usually admit to at least once, sometime, somewhere, when curiosity got the better of them. Granted, you've admitted to the occasional group-grope, but always in safely heterosexual settings. Wouldn't it seem logical that you, subjected as you were – and are – to so much sexual innuendo and same-sex come-ons, would have, at one time or another, with someone, somewhere, said to yourself: 'Everybody figures I'm into this scene. Why not see what it's all about?'"

Like macadamia-cream pie, Dr. Melissa could quickly become too much of a good thing.

I stood.

"Why don't I get back to you on that?" I said. I made sure to note the time: I wasn't about to get overcharged for this one.

Chapter Fourteen

Back in the office the next day, I got a call from Bill the Broker. "There's been some interesting movement in Telaman stock," he said. "Could be a response to our purchases." His "our" told me he had some of his own cash on the line, not that I'd doubted it. "Could be somebody has leaked word of the deZinn book. Could be something else. I've sniffed around. Greenlyne has been in Switzerland a few times this year. A Telaman vice president is over there now."

"What's in Switzerland, besides yodelers and edelweiss?"

"Could be nothing more exciting than a simple 'Hello!' to Steinz Dinst who handles Telaman's European-languages editions."

I'd already drained my brokerage cash account and then some, but I could easily transfer more cash from savings to give Bill additional money to work with. If necessary, he could also convert into Telaman stock any shares in my portfolio that weren't performing up to snuff. I had a feeling about this one. Then again, I'd had hunches before that had brought in zilch – even negative returns.

* * *

I'd called O'Reilly earlier in the day and told him about an unexpected invitation I'd received for the weekend. We agreed to discuss it further in a small, dark cafe-bar just down the block from my building. I commandeered one of the four booths and ordered a cappuccino. I expected O'Reilly to be late, but he was right on time.

He ordered a cup of Roger's Plain Blend brew, black, sugar. "I don't know how you guys drink that stuff," he said and nodded toward my glass in its silver-filigree holder. He didn't say exactly who "you guys" were, but I could guess.

"So, what am I supposed to do about this invitation for the weekend? It's RSVP."

"Tarbothi is fishing, in that he knows you've dabbed most of the holes in the dirty pond."

I couldn't help but wonder at his colorful metaphor. "How much should I tell him?"

"He probably knows everything. What he'll want from you is verification. Did you call Rollins and clear this?"

"Why should I clear it with Rollins? He's not my social secretary."

"I only know what most people would do in your shoes. Caesar might like to know that any hobnobbing with the barbarian at the gates isn't done behind his back."

Actually, I'd talked with Rollins even before I'd called O'Reilly. If Clem had told me to keep clear of Tarbothi, I'd have left O'Reilly out of the loop entirely. "I'd much rather fade out of this bullshit altogether," I said.

"Oh?" O'Reilly didn't believe me any more than Dr. Melissa would have.

"I've a business to run."

"Galin Tarbothi knows a lot of people – good for business."

"You recommend I accept, then?"

"What I'd really like is for you to be in there with a wire."

"No way!"

O'Reilly demurred with what grace he was able to muster. "Doubt if I could get the go-ahead, anyway. Too dangerous for a mere civilian."

If he thought I'd be tempted by the danger involved in such an escapade, he was wrong. Despite what Dr. Melissa believed, white-water rafting, mountain climbing, and polo weren't quite the same as having my guts blown away by some gangster.

"You'll like Tarbothi," O'Reilly went on. "He's all Saville Row, Cerutti-400 shirts, Countess Mara ties, Gucci shoes. Prep school. Ivy League. Fraternities. Cotillions. Low profile. Less rough around the edges than Clem Rollins."

"Who's this Begandi Muffanuffusi who the party is honoring?"

"A Kutani oil minister. Related to the Saudi royal family through marriage. Related to the Brunei sultanate by marriage. Fourteen wives. A Draqual silk nightie, bought by Muffanuffusi for each wife, to be worn only in the harem, for the delight of only Muffanuffusi, could turn you a handsome profit, in exchange for only a couple of days socializing and tennis."

"Who else is going to be there?" I gathered O'Reilly would know. NYPD plants playing "Upstairs, Downstairs" probably.

"The Duke and Duchess of Clencester, pronounced Clenchester, if you please. They've lots of London real estate, and they've hung on to their fortune in spite of a high double-digit percent tax bracket. Bernie Jeaunneaux, a painter. Some canvas that looks as if he defecated on it, not painted on it, recently sold at Sotheby's for a cool six-million-plus. The Freiderich von Peldts. He helped engineer the European Economic Community; she dabbles, most recently in an international company promoting some high-class perfume. The usual down-home folks. You'll fit right in."

"And Guido 'The Shiv' Gortullini?"

O'Reilly actually smiled. "Tarbothi seldom mixes his Perrier with his olive oil, Draqual. Not in the open, anyway. We wouldn't even know he was mob-connected if the CIA hadn't inadvertently targeted him for recruitment while he was in college. Only that pure accident overturned the rock hiding his nefarious past."

I was out of my element and had been from the very start of this conversation.

"Tarbothi is Louie Portucci's bastard," O'Reilly continued. I didn't know any Louie Portucci. "Louie was really low profile. He believed the Mafia could go legit. Ahead of his time. Then and now. And he planned ahead. From the beginning. He put Galin in a maze: big trust fund, right schools, socially correct addresses, old-money marriage. Tarbothi's wife is Helena Cadelma of the Spanish land-grant Cadelmas who once lorded it over half of California."

"This the guy who'd stoop to using a porno tape to topple Clem Rollins?"

"You do what you have to do, Draqual. Sometimes that doesn't necessarily mean deploying the entire US Army and bringing in the whole high-tech arsenal."

* * *

On Friday afternoon, at five o'clock exactly, the doorman buzzed my apartment and told me the Tarbothi limo was waiting.

"Surprise!" greeted Greta Kaney when, at five-oh-six, the Tarbothi chauffeur opened the limo door to reveal her. "I recognized your address, right off."

I scooted in and was engulfed by the combined odors of expensive leather and her expensive perfume. I gave the driver the go-ahead to lower the shade over the glass between the front and back seat. The limo pulled away elegantly from under the porte cochere of my apartment building.

"A pleasant surprise, indeed!" I pretended. "Have you known Galin Tarbothi long, Mrs. Kaney?"

"Hardly at all. I've met him socially a few times. Gerald wanted him for some TV 'Businessman of the Century' broadcast, but it didn't work out. I'm surprised he even remembers me, let alone knew I was in town."

O'Reilly was right again. Damn! Tarbothi was gathering all the major players to verify the viability of his own hand.

"And you, Mr. Draqual?" she asked.

"I?"

"And Galin Tarbothi."

"Don't know the man at all. Invitation courtesy of a friend of a friend of a friend who thought I could use a weekend in the country."

She seemed to accept that at face value. "I was on my way back to Spain when the Tarbothi invitation arrived... since you weren't exactly beating down my door." She looked at me teasingly and sipped from a tulip glass of champagne supplied by the in-car bar.

"You preferred one perfect evening, remember?"

She smiled her pretty, too perfect smile, crossed her two, too perfect legs beneath white linen, and changed the subject. "Wasn't it horrible about Richy Biglow?"

"You knew Biglow?"

"Not as well as Gerald did, but, then, Gerald and Richy had a lot in common."

I had no doubt that what she implied had something to do with big, big men. Also, I had no doubt I'd learn more if I played it stupid. "Oh? How so?"

She seemed amused at my dense stupidity and inability to grasp any immediate connection. "Most of what I know dawned on me after my divorce from Gerald."

I topped off her glass with more champagne and filled a glass for me. The limo ride was as smooth as silk, the driver safely sealed off and hidden from us by shaded glass. The side windows of the passenger salon were smoky-grey one-way glass. I wondered if the car was bugged and, if so, whether it really mattered.

"Gerald and I met Richy Biglow in Japan," Greta went on. "Richy was still at the top of his profession then. Later, he would be in Japan only because it was the only place he could work. I always found it amazing that he was so successful there – of all places. The Asian mind rarely understands Occidental humor, don't you agree?" Like a good hostess, she was prepared to draw my opinions into the conversation.

I knew nothing about Oriental-Occidental comparative humor. "I thought Richy went to Las Vegas," I replied.

"Eventually. After Carson retired. Lounge act only,

though. In Japan, he remained a headliner. I'm always surprised by the number of international show people on Japanese television." Another new topic. Greta was almost as good at quick diversions as Dr. Melissa. "Mainly in commercials, I believe," she continued. "And I'm talking big names who wouldn't be caught dead on American TV, as well as men like Richy Biglow, of course, who have been all but forgotten by most every audience. Done for the money, naturally. Truckloads of it for a time, especially back when Japan was so much the economic powerhouse it pretty much ruled the roost; the Japanese still more than willing to shovel the yen if it means getting someone they're anxious to have hawk their wares. Not for long-life, or for world-wide markets, either, I might add. 'Japan-Only' usually spelled out in the contracts, I think, so that no big star takes the risk of having a US audience see his spiel and think his artistic vision is being compromised for cold, hard cash."

This was quite a lecture – knowledgeable, too. I presumed she had all the facts at hand from her travels around the globe with Gerald.

"Richy wasn't hard up for pocket money, then," I remarked.

"He could live quite comfortably in Japan, outrageously expensive as it still is. Although, he would have preferred star-status in the States, of course."

This was all very interesting, but gossip about the status of Richy Biglow's pocketbook, whether full or lean, veered from what I found of more interest.

"Richy Biglow and Gerald? You say they had a lot in common? Other than show biz, that sounds pretty weird to me." I didn't remember Richy as being particularly fat, but I hadn't seen or heard him perform in years. For all I knew, he may have come to rival the King of Tonga in tonnage. But Greta's pertinent reference had seemed to be of Richy in his prime.

"Gerald and he were extremely keen on sumo wrestling. Richy had some sort of financial investment in one of the top performers. Chu-chu Sansun, or something like that. An enormous man, absolutely huge, but solid as Gibraltar. You've seen sumo wrestling?"

"Only on television."

"Clever TV editing makes it look almost interesting, but it has to be the most boring sport this side of... well, it has to be the most boring sport. Long minutes of inactivity, each wrestler circling the other. Lots of posturing. Foot thumping. Rice throwing. All leading to a few seconds of stomach bumping wherein one fat man eventually knocks a usually less-fat one out of a small, circular ring. One live performance was enough for me, but Gerald and Richy were off to the matches every night... to my utter amazement. I understand the attraction now, of course, but it all would have become clearer to me, faster, if Richy had been more candid in his book. Did you read it?"

"Afraid not." I didn't particularly like clowns, or comics, or mimics...

"It was a Telaman Press book." Now, that was interesting! "It came out a couple of years after we'd traveled in Japan," she went on. "Gerald brought a copy home, autographed: 'To Gerald and Greta who made my Japan the very best!' My part, of course, had been to absent myself obligingly while my husband and Richy drooled over mounds of Oriental blubber. Although, there was nothing about that aspect of travels in old Japan in the book of course. Plenty of other outrageous revelations, though. Richy's affair with Sheila Pennye, for instance. Remember her pendular weight swings? One day, svelte. One day, medium. One day, large. Next day, the Goodyear Blimp. For all her TV audience to see. Again, Stud, I'm being catty, I know, but I can't help but believe that if Richy Biglow made love to her, it was only on her fat days."

Greta leaned back into her corner of the car, uncrossed her legs and then re-crossed them. Nylon sighed against nylon.

The limo sped down the throughway before slowing and turning onto a two-lane road which reached deeper into the countryside. The narrow road was clear, and the car sped up, only to slow again at the outskirts of each small village, with occasional stops at marked crossroads. After more open countryside, the car finally slowed and halted before a gate of twin, ornate, wrought-iron grills, joined along two vertical edges and attended by an appropriately rustic gatekeeper. There was a gate house from which the gate latch was released only after our names had been checked against a list.

The approach road to the house was a twisted, dark drive through trees that could have been survivors of original growth.

"Very nice!" Greta said when she spotted the chateau-like main house as we rounded a bend. A large, finger-shaped lake lie between the house and the road. Beyond the black-mirror water, a huge lawn sloped gently up the far bank, and the house was centered at the top of a distant knoll.

The roadway ran parallel to our side of the lake, then veered to the right over a bridge that looked rooted to the spot with age but which could probably be raised on well-oiled sprockets in case of siege.

After crossing the bridge, the car entered a tunnel of

flowering shrubbery. Mammoth bushes temporarily blocked any additional view of the house until the roadway reached the top of the grade. There, in a swooping right turn, the road spilled on to a gravel court where a large fountain played in the center of a circular flower bed.

Greta and I had each been assigned a separate greeter, respectively female and male.

"Mrs. Kaney."

"Mr. Draqual."

We four entered the house, followed by two younger men carrying our bags. We crossed the black-and-white harlequin-checkered marble floor of a baroque vestibule and climbed the grand staircase to the first landing. From there, Greta was ushered, upward to the right, and I to the left. Silently, we motioned to each other that we'd meet up later.

My suite was large, luxuriously appointed, and overlooked formal gardens which were just visible in the approaching dusk. The man who had ushered me in said: "The guests already arrived are resting in their suites, sir, and Mrs. Tarbothi assumes you, too, might be tired after your journey, as well as a bit hungry. There's a selection of food available. You'll find a menu here on your desk. Dial seven to have something brought up. You may leave the dishes here in your suite, or place them in the hall.

"Breakfast tomorrow will be served in the dining room, between five and eleven." He picked up a glossy printout from the desk. "For your convenience, this is a layout of the house and grounds." (O'Reilly might have welcomed a copy if two floors hadn't been missing from the drawing, as well as several outbuildings I'd seen on the way in).

"Also, for your reference," the usher continued, "here's a listing of the other guests."

The placard contained a photograph of each guest, and mine was pretty good. I couldn't remember having posed for it. Probably cropped from some magazine or newspaper. Under each photo was a job-position designate: "CEO, Draqual Fashions, Inc.", for me; and a roster of that person's preferred extracurricular activities: "white-water rafting, mountain climbing, polo..."

"You'll also note, sir, a list of activities available to you, during the course of the weekend. Horseback riding, sailing, punting, golfing, hiking, croquet, badminton, tennis, squash, bowling (lawn and/or alley), swimming (pool and/or lake), library, game room."

Nor had he yet completed his impressive and perfectly delivered litany: "Lunches will be buffet and will be served in the dining room between noon and four p.m.. Dinner, tomorrow evening, will be black tie at eight, with cocktails at seven, either in the library, or in the drawing room. Sunday's evening meal will be informal and ongoing from five p.m. to accommodate guests wishing to leave early.

"If you need special assistance – sporting equipment, clothing, valet service – please dial nine and ask for me – Wylie."

"Thank-you, Wylie."

"Shall I draw you a bath, sir?"

"Yes, please."

"Very good, sir, and I wish you a pleasant stay."

Well, well, well! A weekend at an English country house it wasn't. That would have been: "You're on your own, old chap, and tie for dinner." This was more a highly organized and deluxe spa where everything and anything was available for the asking, and where no one would think you either too rude or too gauche for the asking.

The bath was large, paneled, in malachite, and, unlike any English country house equivalent, its plumbing was in perfect working order. There were lots of thick towels, a plush robe, bath salts and bath beads.

Once out of my bath, I found that my bags had already been unpacked. This could be either courtesy, or a convenient way of searching all incoming luggage. Who was to know here at Chateau Tarbothi?!

I dialed seven and ordered a supper of cold quail and champagne. As expected, it arrived complete with Irish linen, Tenblock silver, Limoges china and Baccarat crystal.

I plopped into a four-poster bed, canopied in heavily embroidered silk damask, and I was quickly lost to the world.

* * *

The only thing to spoil Saturday morning was the probability of an interrogation by Tarbothi. I got to the dining room fairly early for breakfast, in order to avoid an early-morning run-in with Greta who, I assumed, was a late riser. I wanted to keep myself as free as possible for Tarbothi, if and when he wanted to talk.

I had a pleasant chat with a Mr. Bilkiner who had done his homework. "I did the Rasong Rapids, too," was how he introduced himself. "Nineteen-seventy. Early monsoon made the gorge damned hairy, as you very well know."

In the library, Celia Frasier reminded me that we'd met five years before on a tea plantation in Burma.

"Don't be embarrassed because you don't remember. I was with the Rileys and on my way out, after that horrible sniper incident which killed five of their pickers. You came riding in to find our ragtag bunch on the Salkenbury's front lawn. I told Mandy that I'd never seen a man looking so good in jodhpurs."

I grinned self-deprecatingly, thanked her, and made my escape.

Helena Tarbothi, nee Cadelma, was charming. During the course of the day, she sought me out several times, as she did the other guests, to make me feel welcome. "Galin is anxious to show you his ponies," she said. "He just recently received a really fine specimen from Sheikh Muffanuffusi." I'd yet to spot the guest of honor. "We were uncertain, though, after your unfortunate polo accident..."

"You're very considerate, Mrs. Tarbothi, but I can assure you that I still appreciate magnificent horseflesh."

Galin Tarbothi wasn't neglectful, either. After his initial self-introduction, he, like his wife, talked polo and horses, and he never once referred to Clem Rollins, Jack Fornal, or to Stan Greenlyne. Surprisingly, I got a very strong feeling that Tarbothi thought the mere mention of their names would somehow sully the purity and graciousness of the elegant weekend.

That evening, I dressed for dinner and came down early. I carried my scotch to an outside balustrade which, like my room, overlooked the formal gardens. Tarbothi joined me. He'd not yet dressed for dinner, but he looked tanned and relaxed in a beautifully-cut white linen suit.

"I hope you're not bored with all of this, Mr. Draqual." His nod included his house, grounds, and him.

"Not in the least. I'm delighted to be here."

Tarbothi was a slender six-feet. Thick black hair with no trace of grey. Interesting cheekbones, more Slavic than Mediterranean. A thin, undistinguished nose. Lips full and sensuous. White teeth with predominant canines – a handsomely elegant Count Dracula after nightfall. "No doubt you're aware I'm acquainted with some interesting people. However, there's a particular gentleman I don't know at all... only know of. Made a point to."

Well, now I knew it was going to be the oblique approach. I could only hope it wasn't too oblique.

He continued: "Rhinehold Myerson. CEO, R. Myerson Communications, Zurich. Think you can remember that?"

I repeated the name: "Rhinehold Myerson." I repeated the job title: "CEO, R. Myerson Communications." I repeated the city: "Zurich." A trained mynah I could very easily become.

"Fascinating: the Swiss," Tarbothi said. "Exceptional business acumen. Lots of money to play with. Always looking for somewhere to put it. Even willing to put it into US pastures when those pastures became less green than they once were."

I waited.

"Myerson is a man with whom neither of us should become too familiar," he went on. "Not now, anyway. Might cause complications later. I don't like complications. Not for me. Not for my business. Not for my friends. Not for my business associates."

He started to leave but turned back, momentarily, once he reached the French doors. "Carl Markinson is going back to the City early tomorrow evening. There's a seat in his helicopter if you'd prefer it to the limo."

I'd been fairly advised and fairly warned. "Yes, please."

"The chopper will set down on the pad at seven." Tarbothi smiled. "Mrs. Kaney will be sorry to lose you."

"I rather doubt that," I replied. "She seems to have found Count Teeslindorf."

"I suggest you call your broker from a pay phone in town. We regularly sweep our lines to make sure they're clean, but..." He shrugged. "As far as cell phones, one can never count on their being secure, can one? By the way, my sources tell me, 'it' won't be a done deal until ten a.m. Eastern Daylight Time, Tuesday."

Chapter Fifteen

My weekend at Tarbothi Chateau long over, I actually expected a call. However, this call came at two o'clock in the morning, and it was nobody, on the other end of the line, I recognized.

"Mr. Draqual?"

"Yes." I sat up, switched on the bedside light and squinted into the glare.

"You don't know me, Mr. Draqual." Tell me something I don't know! She obliged with: "My name is Glennis Rhynne."

"I certainly know of you, Miss Rhynne. The police are looking for you, even as we speak... concerning several murders, an attempted murder, and an apparent suicide."

"Yeah, I know."

"I could give you the number of the inspector in charge, name of O'Reilly."

"I'm not talking to the cops, Mr. Draqual, although I've plenty to say. I just thought you might want to hear it before I fade completely into the woodwork."

"Why would I want to hear what you've to say, Miss Rhynne?"

"Don deZinn was your friend, right?"

"I mean, why wouldn't I prefer to hear it from the cops, after they've heard it from you?"

"I'm not talking to the police. I told you."

"But why to me?"

"Paul Cortland thinks you can be trusted."

"You've talked to Paul, then?"

"Not since I told him where Jack was."

"Maybe you'd feel more comfortable saying what you have to say to Paul?"

"Paul has already been fucked over enough by the police, without giving them another excuse. You're not interested, that's fine. We'll leave everything as-is. But there are a few holes that need filling, and I don't know of anyone but me who can do that filling. But I'm not going to ruin what I've planned for myself by risking arrest. I'm not completely innocent in all of this, you know."

"I'm sure the police would cut a deal. Wouldn't you rather have your slate wiped clean than be looking over your shoulder the rest of your life?"

"They're not going to spend too much more time looking for me. Plenty of other cases to keep them occupied. If they can't come up with a motive for Jack, except for some bullshit about him being a hired gun for Clem Rollins, his phony suicide at least wraps up all the packages neatly enough to make most everybody happy. Soon enough, the cops will be happy to shelve it: Case closed."

"Jack's phony suicide?"

"He was killed. Blown away for what he knew. For what I know. By the person who put him up to everything."

"Talk to the cops, Miss Rhynne."

"I won't risk even a day in jail, Mr. Draqual. I had a friend in for only one day. Someone took a knife to her and gave her enough scars on her face to last her – and me – a lifetime." Glennis paused and gathered breath. "She was a whore; I'm a whore. But I don't plan to be a whore much longer. There's enough left from Jack's payoffs for the murders to set me up in a place where no one will ever think of looking. Now, if you want a little chat, before I disappear into my new life, you're welcome. If you're not interested, then I'll at least have offset any pangs of conscience I may have now, or down the road. I do have a conscience, you know!"

"And if I agree to this little chat?"

"Fifteen minutes. The old Jamison Faldwell Theater."

A condemned building for Christ's sake! "Couldn't we meet somewhere more public? An all-night diner? A theater that works? A bar? A disco? A video arcade?"

"I've spent time setting this up, Mr. Draqual. I know the layout. I've an escape route mapped out, in case you get cute and bring the police. I did say not to bring the cops, didn't I?"

"You insinuated as much, yes."

"Promise not to bring them."

I hadn't even decided to bring myself.

She said into the pause: "If you don't show in fifteen, I'll assume you're not interested."

"Wait!" I thought she'd hung up. "Fifteen won't do it, Glennis. I'm in bed. It's two o'clock in the morning. I'd like a quick shower. I have to dress. Get the car. Get to the theater." What other delaying tactic could I come up with?

"You've an hour. No more. And if you come with cops, expect an empty building."

The line went dead.

I threw back the sheet, reached for my pants, and wondered what Dr. Melissa would say.

With time to spare, I parked a block from the Jamison

Faldwell. The surrounding neighborhood had a slasher-movie atmosphere: dark, dirty, and deserted. All that was missing was the name of the horror flick spelled out in big black letters across the cracked, broken, unlit marquee.

I rechecked the immediate area before getting out of the car. Being mugged, en route, wasn't part of the game plan. At least, there were no street-corner gangs of teenage hoods in sight.

My footsteps echoed.

The padlock on the theater door was undamaged, but the hinge to which the lock was secured had been pried loose from the jamb.

The theater lobby was dark and empty. I'd brought the flashlight I kept in my car's glove compartment. Its beam picked up a clutter of splintered lumber, fallen plaster, and cracked tiles. Discarded mad-doper syringes had been discarded, here and there. Fossilized popcorn was scattered over the floor and over the dusty concession counter. Two ramps led into the theater proper. I took the ramp on the right.

I ended up at the back of a huge arena. The floor slanted away from me. Rows of unaligned theater seats were piled, one atop the other, like pick-up sticks. The aisle, that once provided a direct route to the stage, was an obstacle course of debris.

"Draqual?"

I turned my flashlight toward the voice, but Glennis provided her own lighting. She aimed her flashlight beam upward, onto her face, the way kids do when telling scary stories during camp-outs in the backyard. She stood center-stage, backdropped by a curtain which sagged precariously from the few remaining anchors that attached it to a rusted slideway overhang.

"Will the gentleman in the back of the theater please step forward!" Glennis played game-show hostess, which wasn't necessarily reassuring in a deserted theater at three hours after midnight.

I bumped into theater seats, twisted and turned among them, and hopped over all the navigable trash. The closer I came to Glennis, the less confident I was that I had landed in the right place, at the right time. Her hair was a fright wig. Her face looked as if it had been used as a punching bag, just as Paul Cortland had said.

"Take the stairs and meet me behind curtain number one," she said and disappeared in a torrent of rotting curtain material and dust.

The curtain was heavy and encrusted with the kind of filth I'd just as soon not know about. As I pushed through, immense swirls of gunk tumbled from above.

A bank of lights came on. Glennis had, as she said,

certainly been at work setting the scene, and she had proved herself an expert electrician in the bargain. Momentarily, I was blinded by the results. But, there was nothing wrong with my hearing.

"Curiosity killed the cat!" Definitely not Glennis. Definitely not my grandmother.

"Greenlyne, you bastard, is that you?"

"Just stay right there, Draqual!"

There was a loud thump, and Glennis collapsed dramatically into a heap, right at my feet.

Drawn by the blood, seeping through her peroxided hair, I went down on one knee, tilted her head upward, and placed two fingers firmly beneath her jawline. There was a pulse, but a weak one.

"Forget Sleeping not-so-Beauty," Stan's voice was a hiss. He adjusted a two-by-four light support so I was able to see him full-on. He had a gun. "She's served her purpose. Rotten cunt!"

"What's this all about, Stan?" Innocence personified. "You could have called. We could have done lunch."

"Screwed me royally, didn't you, Draqual!?"

"Don't you have me confused with Gerald Kaney, or with Richy Biglow?"

He ignored my obviously too-clever, and decidedly obscene, repartee; he had money on his mind. "I'd be a very rich man if it hadn't been for you."

"The way I hear it, Stan, you were a rich man before Telaman Press was taken over by R. Myerson Communications, Zurich. Even richer afterward."

"How much of that money do you think I'll be able to keep when the Securities and Exchange Commission is through with me?"

"With you? You're a little confused, Stan. I'm the one under investigation by the SEC, remember?"

"You're just the tip of the iceberg, Draqual, and you know it. They're poking their noses into everyone and everything."

"You have nothing to hide... right! Sorry! I forgot."

"Don told you, didn't he? I figured he might, but you didn't rush off to your broker. Not right away. How did you know the takeover wasn't scheduled until later? Don didn't even know, because Gerald didn't know. Gerald didn't know, because I didn't tell him... my way of checking whether the bastard could be trusted. Gerald thought I was talking about a quick return on investment. All I told him was that he might have to wait a little longer than tomorrow. So, Draqual, now I want to know how you got the when, the where, and the by whom?"

"I didn't get them. Certainly not from Don. He was too busy on his book, at a time when I was too busy on a new collection. Once the SEC investigation is over, you'll all see I'm as clean as newly-fallen snow."

"You just acted on a hunch the very day before the deal was done?" He didn't believe it. Can't say as I blamed him. Actually, it was his phone call of complaint for which I'd been waiting when Glennis had surprised with her call.

"Some people luck out on lotteries," I tried. "I lucked out by buying a big block of Telaman stock just before your company was taken over by the Swiss. And, it wasn't as if that day-prior purchase was my only buy. I started picking up Telaman as soon as I suspected you'd lied about a deZinn book still being in the pipeline. You do admit you lied?"

"THE deZINN TAPES, due out this Christmas."

"All I'm saying is that the R. Myerson Communications' takeover caught me completely by surprise."

"You bought too much, too fast, too near to blast-off, for me and the SEC not to smell a rat." Nothing I didn't know. As far as the SEC, it was always being embarrassed by yet another gamut of insider-trading scandals and was always swearing that no one else would slip through the cracks; although, someone always did.

"You, by contrast," I replied, "and in your infinite

wisdom, bought little bits and pieces of Telaman stock, over a very long period. Never in your own name, of course, but by calling in favors from old friends and old lovers, like Gerald Kaney and Richy Biglow. A few shares here. A few shares there. Come the Myerson Communications' takeover time, obliging old friends and old lovers cash in, take commissions, and hand you most of the profits. Wasn't your legitimate share of the deal enough? Millions, wasn't it? All risked for a couple million more?"

"That couple a million more would have been pure gravy, if you hadn't launched your attention-getting buying frenzy."

"You were in trouble long before I arrived on the scene, Stan. Gerald dead. Don dead. Richy Biglow dead. Was it unguarded pillow-talk, to Gerald and Richy, while you were speared on their dicks, of which they took advantage?"

"I liked Gerald. I figured he was happy to buy Telaman shares, cash them in, when the time arrived, and then collect his risk-free commission."

"Then turn the bulk of the money over to you."

"He wouldn't have been an inside player without me. The ungrateful, greedy sonofabitch! Bought the shares I told him to buy. Then bought an even larger block for himself. Bought another block for his bitch of an ex-wife. Then, he blabbed to deZinn."

"I wondered how Don fit it. For awhile, I thought it was chubby-chaser stuff, just never mentioned."

"Gerald... the stupid bastard, drunk as a skunk... told deZinn while recording one of the book tapes. Gerald had to have been brain-dead! Then, forgetting his slip-of-the-tongue was even on it, he turned the tape over to me for transcription. Unbelievable! Gerald with diarrhea of his liquor-loosened mouth. How many more people would he have told? And deZinn, already blabbing out the details of his sex life into a tape recorder, sure as hell wouldn't have had too many qualms about clueing in all his sleazy friends and associates!" Kyle Kaiser popped immediately to mind.

"Why dress two corpses in Draqual silk slips?"

"DeZinn was parading around in his black one when Jack made the hit. I liked the effect, in that it aimed any investigation away from the hallowed halls of the New York Stock Exchange. Jack stole the red Draqual from deZinn's closet, as a present for Glennis; Jack could be generous when he was of a mind and when it didn't cost him anything. But, I rerouted that red piece of Draqual shit to Kaney's corpse, in order to emphasize what had already become, but suddenly became an even better-named, red-herring."

"No Draqual slip, though, for Richy Biglow. Another buddy of yours who decided to cash in on his own?"

"All I gave Richy was a phony promise that Telaman Press would reissue his book. Delusional, he was convinced the reissue would help him make his comeback. Crazy idea! He's more popular dead than he ever was alive and kicking. Telaman's new owners are actually going to reissue the book this October under a new title: DIED LAUGHING. Ain't that cute? Richy's body wasn't supposed to be found. His disappearance was to look, for all intents and purposes, as a last-ditch publicity stunt by a has-been; it was looked on, just that way, too, until the cops got lucky and were tipped off as to the whereabouts of the body."

"Jack Fornal always your trigger man?"

"Handy with a gun, our Jack. All that Army-for-rehabilitation bullshit. I never was all that good, myself. But don't get your hopes up. Even I can manage this gun from this distance."

I ignored his threat. I needed to pump him for information for as long and as hard as I could. "When Jack shoots outside my building, he's not aiming at you, nor is he aiming at me, because he has no intentions of hitting anything but the backseat of your car. The press runs with the story: Don and Gerald dead, you the next target. Something to do with salacious revelations on a tape, from the upcoming deZinn book, putting the CEO of Telaman Press on the firing line. Telaman stock drops, and your friends buy even more at even more bargain prices. More profits to be gained by cash-ins after the R. Myerson Communications' takeover. More grist for the mill when you ask for police protection – and get it! Additional publicity when you refer back to the shooting when the deZinn book comes out at Christmas."

"That's just the gravy. As for the meat and potatoes..."

I waded in even deeper, egged on by his challenge. "What you, likewise, wanted was a diversion to take you off the police's suspect list as far as Gerald's and Don's murders were concerned."

"You're too fuckin' clever for your own good, Draqual. Which I learned only too late. But, you're right. If it appeared that the person who shot deZinn and Kaney then tried to shoot me, police mentality would never come up with the idea that I was the one who hired the gun."

Stan's underestimation of police thinking was as naive as mine had been when all of this started. I'd found out differently, but apparently Stan was still at the bottom of the learning curve.

"The purpose of the fake tape was to point a finger at Clem Rollins as the chief suspect." It didn't hurt me to state the obvious.

"The police could be convinced of Clem's motive for murder," Stan agreed, "and Clem, once he had his hands on the tape, would know that the bit about deZinn and him was a lie, probably concocted by deZinn to make their association appear more interesting, in order to sell more books. Best of all, I'd walk away with the old fart's eternal gratitude for having kept private what I'd seemingly been led to believe was a genuine piece of dirt."

"Why con me into acting as your go-between with Clem?"

"Stretch your mind a little bit farther, Draqual, and come up with your best shot. I'm sure you can see the reasoning, being such a bright little fag!"

It was no time to let myself be provoked by this fat slob. "I knew Clem's wife, and you wanted to appear too genuinely afraid of the truth of what you had in your possession to approach Rollins on your own."

"Only to have you fuck that up, too!"

"Making you one-hundred grand poorer."

"Not too smart of you, Draqual, to throw that in my face. Not with this gun aiming at yours."

I dropped that subject. "You actually thought I wouldn't listen to the tape?"

"What I didn't figure was that you'd recognize the tape as a phony, even if you did listen to it. Richy had made it pretty-near perfect, as far as I could tell." Stan sounded genuinely hang-dog and regretful of this particularly crucial slip-up, as if he wished I'd tell him it was okay, that I understood how he'd had a lot on his mind...

"Why turn the tape over to O'Reilly?" I asked instead.

"I figured you'd blab to O'Reilly about the tape being fake, so giving it to the cops suddenly put me in good stead with them... from uncooperative to here's-what-I've-got. Their electronic equipment would back up what you said about the tape being a fake. Rollins would now be convinced there was a tape, but it was a bogus one... and I'd still end up with bonus points from Clem for not turning the tape over to the cops, until after you'd told everyone it was a forged one.

"Scared the shit out of me, Draqual, when you told me you'd destroyed the tape; Richy dead and unable to do a repeat performance. Rollins wouldn't have been very happy with a missing cassette. With the tape destroyed, he'd never have known, with any real certainty, that it was a fabrication. I never bothered to make a copy for backup, because he certainly would have accessed experts to tell him, right off, that he only had a copy, which would have had him wondering just where the master had gone. To be sure any missing tape was pure bullshit, Rollins might well have hooked me up to a lie detector... or to something worse, like to a cement overcoat – just to get what I knew out of me."

"What about the cops' theory that Tarbothi was out to get Rollins?"

"Didn't do me any harm, did it? And who the hell is this Tarbothi, anyway? All my sources say he's legit."

There was no way I wanted to discuss Tarbothi with Stan Greenlyne, especially now. "What about the anonymous tip to O'Reilly that turned up Richy's body?"

"Courtesy of Jack Fornal and..." Keeping his eyes on me, Stan jerked his head, with no small degree of disgust, toward Glennis who was still sprawled unmoving on the floor. "They letting me know how the two of them had all sorts of cute little tricks they could pull out of their collective hat if I didn't come up with a few more bucks to sweeten their take-home pay. What the stupid fucks didn't realize was that just because I'd hired Jack as a shooter didn't mean I wouldn't have the guts to pull a trigger myself. I'm just wondering if you believe I've got the guts to pull this trigger. If you don't, Draqual, you meddling sack of shit, you guess wrong."

He pulled the trigger, and I felt the bullet slam me with the force of a sledgehammer. The roar echoed through the cavernous theater. I was propelled backward into the curtain which freed itself of its remaining anchors and covered me in a downpour of unbearably filth-heavy shroud.

* * *

I was being slapped gently but firmly on my cheeks. I opened my eyes.

"Atta boy, Draqual! Snap out of it! You're okay. No harm done. Come on, Draqual, take hold! Hey, Pete, help me get this goddamned Devlar vest off him. The fucker can't breathe."

O'Reilly pulled me to a sitting position. He and someone – Pete? – shucked me out of the bullet-proof material. Still in a daze, I looked around me. Stan was nowhere in sight. Glennis was gone, too. Men, who I assumed were plainclothes cops, and a few uniformed police, milled about the cluttered theater arena.

"Well, Draqual, how'd it feel? I have to congratulate you. You did a great job for us! Needless to say, we appreciate it. That bullet pretty much destroyed the wire you were wearing, but you'll be glad to know that, while you were pumping Greenlyne for information, all the good stuff was simultaneously broadcast to recording equipment in a van outside. Even got the sound of the revolver going off. Nearly deafened the poor rookie who was doing the listening."

I didn't mention that Stan could just as well have shot me in the head where, from where I'd been standing, he'd seemed to be aiming. Why taint the joy of an already won game?

Chapter Sixteen

SECURITY EXCHANGE COMMISSION: "Would you state your full name, including any middle name or middle-initial-only."

DRAQUAL: "Stud Draqual."

SEC: "Have you ever had occasion in the last year to analyze Telaman Press?"

DRAQUAL: "Yes."

SEC: "What was the first occasion within the last year that you analyzed Telaman Press?"

DRAQUAL: "Shortly prior to my first major purchase of Telaman Press stock as referenced in Exhibit A."

SEC: "And how did it happen that you first began to analyze Telaman Press?"

DRAQUAL: "I had the idea that Telaman Press might have sufficient materials on hand to publish a book Don deZinn was doing for them prior to his murder."

SEC: "When did you first get this idea?"

DRAQUAL: "Just prior to my first purchase of Telaman Press stock. That was when it first actually jelled. It had been vaguely in the back of my mind ever since Mr. deZinn's murder."

SEC: "To what do you attribute this idea?"

DRAQUAL: "I guess to my awareness of just how long Mr. deZinn had been working on his book prior to his murder. It seemed sufficiently long enough to have produced something viable."

SEC: "Did you ever discuss the progress of this book with Mr. deZinn?"

DRAQUAL: "I don't remember. I was busy at the time, but we spoke on occasion. If he did mention it, which I suppose he must have, I'm sure it was only in generalities."

SEC "He never said, 'I've finished my book'? Or, 'I'm on the last chapter of my book'? Or, anything to lead you specifically to believe he was nearing completion of, or had actually completed, his book?"

DRAQUAL: "He did not."

SEC: "Have you ever had any contact with Mr. Stan Greenlyne?"

DRAQUAL: "Yes."

SEC: "In what connection?"

DRAQUAL: "Prior to Mr. deZinn's death, I met Mr. Greenlyne socially on several occasions. After Mr. deZinn's murder, Mr. Greenlyne approached me to arrange a meeting between Mr. Clem Rollins and him."

SEC: "Regarding the deZinn book?"

DRAQUAL: "Regarding one of the tapes Mr. deZinn had made for reference, while writing his book. Rather, a tape which was assumed to have been one used as reference for the deZinn book. It was later proven to be a forgery."

SEC: "At any time, during your contact with Mr. Greenlyne, did he ever mention to you that he had enough material to publish the deZinn book?"

DRAQUAL: "Not until after I'd liquidated all of my Telaman Press shares. Before that, he'd made it a point to insinuate there wasn't enough material available for a book. That can be verified from Mr. Greenlyne's statements, made just prior to his arrest, included in the police transcripts I've made available as Exhibit B."

SEC: "At any time during your contact with Mr. Greenlyne did he ever mention a buy out of Telaman Press?"

DRAQUAL: "Not until after the fact."

SEC: "Did Mr. Greenlyne ever mention R. Myerson Communications, Zurich?"

DRAQUAL: "Not until after the fact."

SEC: "No mention whatsoever?"

DRAQUAL: "None. I again refer you to the statements Mr. Greenlyne made just prior to his arrest, as transcribed from police tapes, and made available to you as Exhibit B."

SEC: "You placed three substantial orders to buy Telaman Press stock. The last, a very large order, being one day prior to the announcement by R. Myerson Communications, Zurich, that it was making a tender offer for Telaman Press stock."

DRAQUAL: "Yes."

SEC: "Which you attribute purely to luck."

DRAQUAL: "To luck, yes, and to my broker having noticed telltale spurts of activity in the trading of Telaman Press shares."

SEC: "Your broker would be Mr. William Kavan of Kavan, Wilhelm and Ascondin."

DRAQUAL: "Yes."

SEC: "Did Mr. Kavan ever mention to you that he had information to the effect that Telaman Press was going forward with the deZinn book?"

DRAQUAL: "No."

SEC: "Did Mr. Kavan ever mention to you that he had information to the effect that any company whatsoever was interested in taking over Telaman Press?"

DRAQUAL: "No."

SEC: "Did Mr. Kavan ever make any mention of R. Myerson Communications, Zurich?"

DRAQUAL: "No."

SEC: "All of your decisions to buy Telaman Press shares were your own?"

DRAQUAL: "After I made my first purchase, I believe Mr. Kavan reported what he thought to be unaccounted-for movement of Telaman Press stock. But he couldn't pinpoint any reason why this should be so. I don't believe one could call that a recommendation to buy. In fact, I'm sure it wasn't. It was merely a passing of information, since he knew I was interested."

SEC: "Do you remember if you bought Telaman Press shares on the basis of this specific conversation with Mr. Kavan?"

DRAQUAL: "I bought Telaman Press shares, but not specifically because of that conversation. I was interested in Telaman Press. I'd already bought Telaman Press shares, and I simply decided to buy more."

SEC: "Not knowing of the proposed R. Myerson Communications, Zurich, move on Telaman Press?"

DRAQUAL: "Yes, not knowing. My idea at the time was centered only on the possibility of publication of the deZinn book; that idea stayed with me despite Mr.

Greenlyne's insinuations to the contrary. Mr. Kavan's report of possible movement in Telaman Press shares indicated to me that insider word of the deZinn book might have leaked, to those in position to buy, before any concrete announcement was made to those of us in the general public."

SEC: "Did you know that Mr. Kavan made purchases of Telaman Press shares for his personal account which mirrored each of your own larger purchases?"

DRAQUAL: "Only insofar as I know that Mr. Kavan has played hunches before."

SEC: "Did you ever discuss his personal purchases with him?"

DRAQUAL: "No."

SEC: "Are you aware of any other stock purchases, not necessarily of Telaman Press shares, that Mr. Kavan has made on your recommendation, or on information you might have given to him?"

DRAQUAL: "No."

SEC: "Did you at any time mention anything to Mr. Kavan about the deZinn book?"

DRAQUAL: "I mentioned that I thought a deZinn book was likely, based on the length of time Mr. deZinn had been working on it. I had no concrete facts, however, except the contradictory ones surrounding Mr. Greenlyne's insinuations that there wasn't going to be a book."

SEC: "Did you ever mention R. Myerson Communications, Zurich, to Mr. Kavan?"

DRAQUAL: "I was unaware of R. Myerson Communications, Zurich, at the time."

SEC: "When exactly did you become aware of R. Myerson Communications, Zurich?"

DRAQUAL: "When it announced its tender offer for Telaman Press shares."

SEC: "Did Inspector John O'Reilly, NYPD, ever mention R. Myerson Communications, Zurich, to you?"

DRAQUAL: "No."

SEC "Did Inspector O'Reilly ever insinuate that Telaman Press was prepared to publish the deZinn book?"

DRAQUAL: "As I recall, the book was mentioned by Inspector O'Reilly, but only in a speculative what-if context: What if the fake tape hadn't been discovered? What if the information on the tape had been transcribed? What if the misinformation had been published?"

SEC: "Did Inspector O'Reilly ever state that Telaman Press would publish the deZinn book?"

DRAQUAL: "No. I remember that I asked him outright if that were the case. He said he was unable to comment, either way. Or, something to that effect."

SEC: "If we could briefly review your orders to buy:

Fifteen-thousand shares of Telaman Press at seventeen dollars and twenty-five cents per share.

Twenty-eight thousand shares of Telaman Press at seventeen dollars and fifty cents per share.

Two-hundred-sixteen-thousand shares of Telaman Press at eighteen dollars per share.

In summation: a grand total of two-hundred-fifty-nine-thousand shares of Telaman Press at an average of seventeen dollars and fifty-eight cents per share."

DRAQUAL: "That's correct."

SEC: "R. Myerson Communications, Zurich, went public, with a twenty-seven dollars per share tender offer for Telaman Press stock, the day following your last order to buy. Within a week, you cashed in your total holdings of two-hundred-fifty-nine-thousand shares of Telaman Press, at an average per-share price of twenty-two dollars and forty-five cents."

DRAQUAL: "That's correct."

SEC: "For a profit in excess of one-million dollars."

DRAQUAL: "Yes."

Epilogue

The following is the text of an advertisement appearing in the Sunday, December _th, edition of "The New York Times Book Review":

This Christmas, don't miss the next blockbuster from Telaman Press!*

THE KILLER INSIDE
by Stan Greenlyne

The first-person account of insider killings, literal and figurative, among the high-stakes players on Wall Street. By the man who lived them and went to death row because of them.

---

*Telaman Press is a registered trademark of R. Myerson Communications, Zurich.